Lewis Cannon

R.R.R.

Rogue River Roy
and
Young Matt McCoy

by Dr. Lewis R. Cannon B.S.

ISBN: 978-0-9793514-2-6
First Printing March 2007

WEGFERDS' PRINTING & PUBLICATIONS
Cover by Karen Wegfahrt
North Bend, OR 97459

Printed in the U.S.A.

ABOUT THE AUTHOR

Lewis Cannon was born in Gold Beach Oregon, on July Fourth, 1923, amid the fireworks that were to set the stage for the rest of his life. Lewis was a Rogue Scholar as he spent more time fishing than he did in school. Fishing the river was his first love, followed closely by setting off explosives. (He never mixed the two.)

Lewis started out small putting firecrackers under tin cans. He loved to see them blown high into the sky. Next came a marble gun followed by a cannon. It was made out of the axel housing from a Model "T". It fired green plums over two hundred yards.

When he was a senior in high school he accidentally blew up the chemistry lab. The principal told him he would still graduate if he promised to leave town. It was an agreement made by the town council.

The only known photograph of Lewis as a young man was taken with the chemistry class; he's the one with the blackened face. Lewis was saved by a tragic event far out in the Pacific on December 7, 1941. He joined the army and was immediately assigned to the Combat Engineers as a Demolition Expert.

At the end of World War II he elected to stay in the army, where he would be paid to blow things up.

In March of 1952 he was sent to Korea and was wounded in action fighting on the 'Hook'. Lewis was honorably discharged in 1954, as a result of his war wounds.

Next Mr. Cannon attended the University of Oregon, M.I.T., Harvard, Yale and Princeton. Dr. Cannon received his fourth doctorate from the University of Colorado working at J.I.L.A., The Joint Institute of Laboratory Astrophysics. (Where he *didn't* blow up the lab.) The good doctor was then recruited by the C.I.A. and disappeared until 1988, when he retired to Gold Beach, Oregon.

Using his C.I.A. and computer skills he erased all his previous records then vanished. He can be reached by placing an ad in the classified section of The World, in Coos Bay, Oregon. It must read, "Have box of wooden kitchen matches, Phoenix brand, used only once." Include your phone number or E-Mail address.

Rogue River Roy

DEDICATION

I would like to dedicate this book to the "Four Juries" a Coos Bay critique group for generously giving of their time and talents in the writing of this story.

And last as always, for Patricia Melvin for her countless hours of diligent work, with love and thanks.

With love and gratitude
I. F. Hessler

Prologue

Little Matt stood alongside the dusty road as the stagecoach pulled away with a clatter of hooves and squeak of harness. Both hands clutched a small carpet bag held in front of him. It contained everything he had left in the world. The valise wasn't the only heavy burden the small lad carried.

He was a stranger to the ways of this new rugged land. It had been a long dusty ride all the way from Flat River, Missouri to the coast of Oregon Territory. Twenty-eight days of mud, dust, heat and cold. Through rugged country, the likes of which he had never seen before.

Mountains, deserts, forests and narrow trails cut through deep canyons with raging rivers far below. He was accustomed to lazy, dun colored rivers that moved so slowly you couldn't tell which way they were flowing, unless you threw in a twig and watched it drift.

Matt had held onto the leather strap so tight it made his hands ache. He was afraid to look at the white water in the pit of the canyons far below, but couldn't help himself.

The driver had thrown down the boy's bag in a cloud of dust and said, "Stay put till your uncle comes to fetch you. If you wander off a cougar'll have you for supper. Be shore'n tell Roy 'howdy' from Willie."

The coach was gone before he could ask what

a cougar was, probably like a catamount or something. At the barber shop in town, back in Missouri, he had seen the musty, moth eaten head of a stuffed mountain lion, his teeth still frightening even in death. He shuddered at the thought and wondered where his uncle was.

A tree just off the road looked like a good place to set his grip and wait a spell. As he bent over to put his belongings down something hit him on the backside. Matt looked around quickly . . . there was no one in sight.

Dust from the long journey covered him from head to toe. Using his cap he began dusting off his clothes. It was like a little miniature dust storm swirling away on the wind. When he bent over to dust his shoes, something hit him on the backside, again!

"Ouch!" He cried out, rubbing his butt.

A shrill voice came out of the sky, "You're the dirtiest boy I ever saw!"

Matt looked in the direction the rock must have come from and asked, "Who said that? Show yourself ... coward!"

A little giggle came from the branches of a tree across the road.

"I'm not kidding! Show yourself or I'll chuck this rock at you!" He said, as he picked up a good throwing stone.

The branches parted and a red headed, freckle faced, imp appeared.

The head spoke, "You're new here. Where are you from? Why do you dress so funny? How come you're all alone? How old are you? You're just a kid like me. Where'd you get those funny shoes?"

The sound of a distant cow bell rang sternly and stopped her chatter abruptly.

"That's Ma! Time for supper."

She scampered down the tree and was through the barb-wire fence in a flash, running off towards a large farmhouse across the meadow, her blue dress blowing in the wind.

She called back, "My name is Cat, short for Cathleen," as she disappeared into the tall grass.

"I'm Matt," he replied, his voice trailing off . . . he doubted she heard him.

He sat down and leaned back against the tree, his stomach started to grumble at the thought of a table of steaming delicious food. It had been over a month since he had eaten a home cooked meal. The stage stops had food the driver called swill or gruel, it must be another name for stew or mush. It was ten cents a plate for children under ten, so he was nine. The only meal he really liked was breakfast. Mostly they served bacon, eggs and biscuits, that was, if the eggs weren't runny. Most of the hot-cakes, Willie said, you could use to shingle a barn if you could manage to drive nails through 'em. He liked Willie, the driver, but he always seemed to be in a hurry.

The sun had set and the penetrating dampness of the coast was now assaulting him as a foggy mist started to roll in. He gathered a handful of rocks and pitched them at one of the fence posts, but soon tired of his game.

Where was his Great Uncle Roy? He should

have been here hours ago . . . . He had never ever seen his uncle, only a fading face in a silver picture frame on the mantle. It was a picture of a young man and woman with two little children that must have been taken long, long ago. He was wearing a gray, soldier's uniform with a hat in one hand and the other on the shoulder of his wife. A cavalryman's sword dangled from his belt. The woman was seated on a chair with two small children standing in front of her. His Uncle Bartholomew had sent the photograph along with him so Matt could give it to his Uncle Roy.

An owl hooted nearby startling the young traveler. A gust of wind rustled some dry leaves and a branch cracked in the darkness. The hair on the back of his neck rose. Matt stifled a cry; he must be a big boy as his mother had always told him. Maybe he should go to the farm house he thought, but it was so dark now he was afraid to move.

A lamp was burning in a lower window of the house giving a yellow cast to the blackness, but little comfort.

The young man shivered in the darkness as he opened his carpet-bag to get a sweater to put on under his coat.

Suddenly he heard chickens squawking, a door opened casting a beacon into the night. A lantern bobbed past the house then a shout! Two whumphs from a shotgun, a muted @#$%&*. The door opened, again spilling out the light, then snipped it off as it closed. Darkness and silence followed.

Goose bumps covered Matt as he sat and

wondered what happened. Next he thought he heard a rustling close by in the grass! He froze with fear . . . . Afraid to move he remained motionless for the longest time.

Once again he felt a chill as a shudder went through his frail body. As he pulled the wool sweater over his head he thought he head a women cry out. Then with his ears uncovered he listened, but couldn't hear anything except the wind in the trees. He was on the verge of tears.

What was keeping his Uncle Roy? He pondered as he pulled his collar up and his hat down as a hedge against the dampness.

"I wish he would get here." His tiny voice said, into the night.

A lantern came floating across the field toward him. As it came closer the outlines of a woman with a shotgun and a young man holding the light were seen more clearly. They headed right for the tree where Matt was sitting. When they got to the fence the young lantern holder put his foot on the middle strand of barb-wire and pushed down, with his free hand he pulled up on the top one. The woman broke the double barrel shotgun, gathered her skirts and stepped through the opening.

As she straightened up she closed the action and said into the dark, "Hello! Are ye still here youngster?"

Matt stood up much relieved and said, "Yes Mam."

The young man with her said, "Look at this Ma," as he pointed out a tuft of fur snagged on a barb.

"Hold the lantern over here Shaun," the woman said, as she bent over and examined some tracks in the thick dust near the edge of the road. Sure enough there was a large cat track with one toe missing.

"So it was 'Old Three Toes' we're going to have to set a trap for that scoundrel and real soon. We've lost enough chickens and lambs to that wily critter. We best get another dog too. We didn't have this much trouble when old Red was alive."

She turned her attention back to Matt and said, "Come along son ye can't stay out here alone. I'll fix ye some vittles and a corner to sleep in."

Matt was so tired, hungry, cold and scared, mostly scared, he was grateful for the invitation.

"I'm Mrs. Murphy and this is me oldest boy Shaun and you be ...?"

"I'm Matt ... Matt McCoy from Missouri, Mam." Not forgetting his manners he added, "Pleased to meet 'cha."

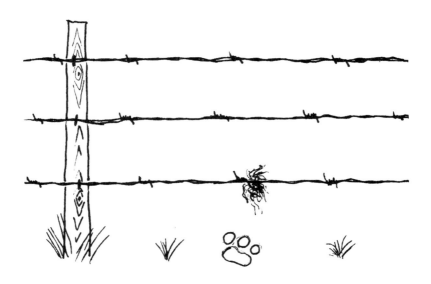

Chapter One

GUN PLAY AT THE GREEN LANTERN

The little town of Gold Beach was quiet as Roy led his string of pack mules down the dusty main street, headed for the Green Lantern Saloon and Public Eatery. He staked them in a small field near Dan's Hardware Store and gave each of them an apple to keep them content while he was gone. It had been about three months since he had stopped at the café and his mouth watered at the thought of a piece of pie and a mug of milk.

The locals called him Rogue River Roy and almost everyone knew him. He had been traveling the roads and trails of the river valley for some twenty years.

He was kept busy hauling supplies and mail to ranchers, miners, homesteaders and farmers all along the rugged frontier valley. It didn't seem like it had been a quarter of a century since the War Between the States had ended. He still woke at night, in a sweat, dreaming about some of the fearful battles he had fought. The nightmares came less frequently now as the memories faded. Only time could heal the mental wounds of war.

Roy brought news along with his goods, but never gossip. He didn't talk about his friends only to them face to face.

It was just before noon as Roy bounded up the steps to the boardwalk and pushed through the swinging doors, pausing for a moment to let his eyes adjust to the dim light. There was a vacant table in the far corner of the main room, past the pot-bellied stove and Roy made a bee-line for it. He caught Ma's eye and pointed to the table and she nodded yes.

She put down the coffee pot wiped her pudgy hands on her ever present apron and headed for Roy's table to take his order.

"I'll have some of your fine blackberry pie and a mug of milk if it's not too much bother." Roy said.

"Shucks no! I'm always happy to serve you Roy. You're one of the few gentlemen I like to attend to." She said with a wink.

Roy looked around the large room used both for drinking and eating, with the usual card game going on at one of the back tables. He nodded at a few men he knew and noticed more strangers than normal, but that was to be expected in a growing western town.

Joe, the bartender, was polishing the bar. He looked over held up a shot glass and smiled. He knew the old man seldom took a drink. Roy shook his head no as he took off his old battered hat and placed it on a vacant chair.

Drinking was something the old man had

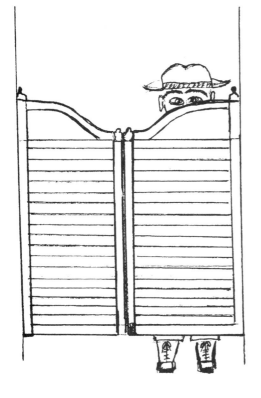

given up many years ago not too long after the war. It didn't solve any of his problems or dull the memories of that dreadful conflict. Besides when you were drunk anyone could rob you or worse and in a rough town you could end up dead.

In a few minutes the milk and pie arrived, he thanked Ma and started in before the plate quit moving. He'd been thinking about having a slice of blackberry pie ever since he passed the ferry landing.

BANG! . . . Both swinging doors hit the walls at the same time. A tall stranger burst through them. He was dressed all in black from his hat to his boots, with the exception of a red bandanna that flared in the light coming over his shoulder. Standing, silhouetted in the opening his emotionless eyes took in the whole room at a glance. With a clank of spurs he strode to the bar and in a deep, whispery voice said, "Whiskey."

Joe popped the cork off a bottle and slid a shot-glass down the polished bar to the stranger then stepped over and poured him a slug of whiskey.

The tall man picked up the drink and slammed it on the bar hard enough to shatter the glass.

"Now pour me a whiskey and fill it to the top, or I'll slam you on the bar." The man's expressionless eyes didn't change nor did he raise his voice.

With shaking hands Joe poured as he was told and stepped back bottle still in hand.

"Leave the bottle!" the stranger ordered through clenched teeth.

Roy noticed Stumbly the town drunk and sweeper leave through the side door.

He's either scared or going for the sheriff, Roy thought.

The somber man stood with one foot on the brass rail as he downed his drink in one gulp, grimaced and then gazed around the silent room taking in every face in turn. His dark eyes stopped when they came to Roy.

"Those mules outside belong to you, old man?" the stranger asked.

Roy pretended he didn't hear the gunslinger and just kept eating his pie without looking up.

"I'm talking to you old man - you in the corner!" the agitated drifter said loudly.

Roy still ignored him trying to draw him closer.

There was a scraping of chairs as everyone moved away from Roy, not wanting to get caught in the bight of the line. Roy pretended he didn't notice, his attention was focused on his pie.

The tall man crossed the room and towered over the seated mule skinner.

"I said . . ."

"Yep, they sure do." Roy said, interrupting the gunman, still not looking up.

"The only thing dumber than a mule skinner is two mule skinners," he challenged.

Roy noticed the man's voice became a little higher-pitched.

"I've no quarrel with you stranger. I'm only here to eat my pie and be on my way."

"You the hombre they call Rogue River Roy?" the tall man asked as he moved his coat aside exposing his six gun.

"Who want's to know?"

"Vince Vermilion, that's who! You killed my brother now I'm here to even the score," he said shrilly.

Roy swallowed hard, not because of the pie, and said, "I didn't kill him. I turned him over to the sheriff."

"Yah and the sheriff hung him and I blame you. Now fill your hand with iron or die trying!" Vermilion said, working himself into a rage.

Just then the swinging doors banged open as Sheriff Smith entered the saloon. He paused in the doorway . . . a shadow outlined in a shaft of light. His star gleamed in the lamplight. Smith squinted into the dimly lit interior as his hands hovered over his matched Colt .44's!

Roy figured Vermilion was going to draw on the sheriff the instant he spotted his badge. It was up to him to stop the sheriff from being killed.

The outlaw made a move to his revolver. Before he cleared leather Roy's fork was in the back of his hand! A look of surprise and pain flared in the killer's cold eyes.

With his left hand Vermilion went for his hideout gun, but the old man was faster! The duel bark of Roy's .41 Derringer surprised the gun fighter. A look of disbelief showed in his eyes. He stared down at the blossoming wound, a realization of death flashed across his face. The gunman staggered and fell backwards his back-up revolver fired harmlessly toward the tin ceiling. A shower of glass from the shattered chimney of an overhead lamp fell to the rough boards. One of the west's cruelest desperadoes lay dead on the saloon floor.

Roy caught a movement out of the corner of his eye and turned his head just as Sheriff Smith pitched forward on his face, hands on his still holstered guns.

One of the dance hall girls screamed, "The sheriff's been shot!"

The bartender was the first one to reach the lawman and rolled him over on his back. He had a bloody gash about three inches long above his left ear, but he was still breathing.

"Must'a been a ricochet got him," Joe said.

Roy was bending over the fallen lawman when the doors opened cautiously in squeaky protest. The sheriff's deputy stepped in timidly with his gun in his hand. It was pointed at Roy!

"Drop that shooting iron mister! Now!" the new deputy said.

Roy suddenly realized he still had his Derringer in his hand and dropped it like a hot branding iron.

"Now unbuckle that gun-belt real slow and let it fall . . . slow now!"

"What are you doing Deputy Butts, this is Rogue . . . ."

"Shut-up Joe or I'll run you in too," the arrogant young deputy said.

Roy heard the sheriff had hired another lawman to help with the newcomers that the gold strike had drawn in, but this was the first time he'd any dealings with him.

Ma was a kind, hard working woman, but when she saw the new deputy was going to arrest Roy, she lit into him with language from the devil's dictionary. She started out by calling him a stupid overbearing jackass with questionable heritage and it went down hill from there.

The young lawman then threatened to arrest her for interfering with matters that didn't concern a woman.

That was the last straw; she was so red-faced mad she headed for the bar to get Joe's sawed off shotgun.

Roy said, "Hold on Ma, I have a favor to ask of you. My great nephew is due to arrive on the stage at the Murphy place and it doesn't look like I'll be able to meet him. I sure would be obliged if you could get word to their ranch and have them take him in. If you're in jail you won't be able to help me."

Ma stopped - the rage showing in her eyes diminished a little, but she was still shaking. "Of course Roy," she said, simmering down. "I'll be glad too. How old is the little tyke?"

"I reckon he's about nine or ten now, just lost his ma and pa to the fever. I got a letter about three months ago from a lawyer in Flat River, Missouri, telling me he was sending my great nephew out on the stage coach. I asked Whip'em Willie the driver to keep an eye out for him and to drop him off by Murphy's. I planned on being there, but with this business it doesn't look like I'll make it."

"Black Cloud is supposed to be camped south of town on Hunter Creek; maybe you could send someone out and tell him what's going on." He added.

"Come along old timer and don't give me any of your sass you're going to jail," said the new deputy.

Chapter Two

MEANWHILE BACK AT THE RANCH

When Matt entered the Murphy ranch house it was filled with light, noise, people and good smells. Such a contrast to the loneliness he had been feeling sitting under the tree by the road in the dark cold night.

There were boys and girls of all ages, each smiling, talking and engaged in some activity. The biggest boy started to clean the shotgun with hot water, a middle girl was reading to a younger boy, while the rest were setting a long table with wonderful smelling food.

Mrs. Murphy was in the center of it all giving orders and guiding all the hustle and bustle. She told Matt to remove his shoes, take off his cap and coat and make himself ta' home.

To the left of the kitchen range, just past the wood box, was a spindle backed rocking chair. Mrs. Murphy chased the cat off and said, "Sit here Matt."

He sat there with his legs swinging watching the children stealing glances at him. He was having trouble keeping his eyes open in the warmth of the kitchen after being out in the chill of the evening.

The sound of a horse galloping up to the front of the house brought everything to a stand still. In the silence they heard the squeaking of boards as someone crossed the porch then a knock on the door.

"Everyone back to work," Mother Murphy said, as she nodded to her oldest child, "See who's at the door."

Shaun, with the reassembled shotgun in his hand, opened the door cautiously and peered into the night. He arched back quickly, startled by the sight of an old Indian inches from his face.

"Good evening young man I have a message for your mother, is she home?" the old Indian inquired in a soft voice.

"Who is it son?" his mother asked, as she came to the door.

"It's Cloud, he says he has a message for you," still somewhat shaken.

"Why bless my soul if it isn't Mr. Black Cloud. Come right in and make yourself ta' home. It must be six months since ye stopped by to see us. Now what was this about a message?"

"Roy's in jail and can't pick up his nephew at the stage stop and was wondering if you couldn't oblige him and keep the lad until he's able to make it here his name is . . . ."

"Matt," Mrs. Murphy interrupted, "he's already here. Cathleen told me there was a boy up by the road waiting for someone to pick him up. When we heard the cougar after the chickens we fetched him in, that's him asleep in the chair. Com'on in we're about to have supper and you're welcome to join us sir."

"Sheila wake up young Matt and get him washed up for supper and set a place for Mr. Black Cloud," Mrs. Murphy ordered. Now what's this about Roy being in jail?"

"The sheriff's been shot and that new bonehead deputy has arrested Roy as the shooter." The Indian informed her.

"Oh my!" She exclaimed, "I don't believe it! Roy would never do anything like that."

"The stupid thing about it was the deputy didn't even notice the body across the room amongst the tables and chairs. It was Vince Vermilion! The most dangerous outlaw in the Oregon Territory." The old Indian told her. "Now if that don't beat all."

"Lands sakes," declared Mrs. Murphy, "was Roy hurt?"

"No Mam he didn't get a scratch. He's just angry and can't believe the smugness of the new deputy. I wouldn't be surprised if he comes up with a PLAN for the greenhorn lawman. Doc Plaster said Sheriff Smith should be back on his feet in a day or two. He was only grazed." Black Cloud told her.

Matt sat uncomfortably at the large, food laden table he had a feeling everyone was looking at him and of course they were - he was new. The youngster couldn't stop staring at the old Indian who smiled back with knowing eyes.

At home he had always been told, 'Children should be seen and not heard.' He had not been allowed to talk at the dinner table only answer questions when asked. *Here* everyone seemed to be talking at the same time.

He was asked about his trip to Oregon on the stagecoach . . . so many questions he hardly had time to eat.

Sheila asked, "Aren't your parents worried about you traveling all alone out in the Wild West?"

"They're both dead." he whispered.

It was the first time he had said it. He sat there. Tears began to well up in his eyes and he lowered his head hoping no one would notice. Matt was ashamed they were dead and didn't know why he felt that way. There was silence at the table, only the sharp click of dishes and silverware.

Mrs. Murphy tried to break the silence, she said to Matt, "We have been asking all the questions, isn't there anything you are curious about child? Go ahead and ask us anything you'd like."

Matt looked up and said, "Why is there an empty chair at the head of the table, a place set and no one there?"

All eight of the red-headed children looked at their mother wondering what she would say.

"Well child . . . about three years ago Mr.

Murphy left on a trip to San Francisco to take some money to his brother Martin. It was his part of an inheritance from his dear departed papa. We haven't had a word from him since."

"To show we haven't given up on him we set a place and leave a light in the window every night." The dark haired woman said.

"Do you know where my uncle is? He was supposed to meet me and I don't know what happened to him." Matt asked.

"Lands sake child, he's in jail. Ye must' a been washing up or asleep when Mr. Cloud gave us the news."

Matt dropped his fork with a clatter a look of panic on his young face, "In jail? He was supposed to take care of me."

What kind of a grown-up is this? Who have I been sent to live with? I've never known a man that's been in jail before, he thought.

"Don't fret yourself son everything will work out just fine." Mrs. Murphy said, as she reached over and patted the back of his hand. "Your uncle stays with us most of the time when he's not out gallivanting through the wilderness. I'll bet he intends for you to stay here too and didn't have time to make the arrangements."

"This is a big house Mr. Murphy and his brother built for us, we have plenty of room and would be happy to have you . . . why you could share young Nathaniel's bed, he's about your age."

Young Nate looked at Matt and smiled mischievously, nodding yes.

The leather faced Indian spoke at last, "Your Uncle Roy has been my friend for over twenty years and if I had a son I would want Roy to raise him. I think that much of him." With that said, he went back to eating. He was one to load-up on good cooking when the opportunity was presented.

Matt stared at the old Indian he knew he wasn't supposed to ask an adult a question, but his curiosity got the better of him. "How come you don't talk like an Indian?" His own voice surprised him.

There was a twinkle in Black Cloud's dark eyes as he answered him, "I was raised by French Missionaries back East - 'many moons ago', he said with a laugh. They were very strict and slapped the back of our hands with a ruler, if we did not know our lessons. But I'll tell you all about it sometime when we're on the trail."

On the trail! Was I going on the trail? Matt sat silently toying with his supper as he digested the new information.

The idea of staying in this busy house full of children sounded like a lot of fun and Matt smiled at the thought.

Another pair of Irish eyes smiled also at the idea of one another young boy to torment. Cat was pleased.

Chapter Three

THE BLACK HAND

Roy woke early the next morning, having spent an uncomfortable night on the bare boards of a jail house bunk. His bones ached and his stomach growled, *it was hell to get old,* he thought. He sat on the edge of his cot and watched the shadow of the bars in his window slide slowly across the wall as the sun moved south. After about an hour he started to yell for some water.

When the young deputy finally woke and answered his call, he brought a dipper of water and was passing it through the bars just as there was a loud kick at the door. He dropped the dipper as he drew his revolver clumsily and said, "Who's there?"

"It's Ma! . . . with a tray of food, now open up or I'll throw it out," the agitated woman said, as she gave the door another kick.

The deputy holstered his gun, opened the door and put out his hands to accept the tray of sausage, eggs, biscuits and a pot of steaming coffee.

"Step back - Squeaky - this ain't for the likes

of you," Ma said, as she brushed past the lawman giving him a defiant look.

"Now open that cell door so I can feed this poor starving gentleman."

"What did you call me when you came in?" the law man demanded.

"Squeaky," Ma said, 'cause of the way you opened those swinging doors last night. Everyone in town is calling you Squeaky, Squeaky Butts, the Dope'dy Sheriff," She laughed giving him a wicked look.

Roy snickered and then covered his mouth with his bandanna, but you could still see the merriment in his eyes. He then managed to ask how Sheriff Smith was doing this morning. Ma told him he was still unconscious, but Doc Plaster said he'd probably come around in a day or two.

"You don't have all day old man now finish up real quick you got a date with the judge," the disgruntled lawman said.

*   *   *

Judge Whitehead looked up over his reading glasses when the sounds of rattling chains entered his courtroom. There was a look of astonishment on his face. "Is that you Roy?" he asked. "Deputy what is this man doing in chains? Release him at once!"

"But your honor this man . . . ."

"I said release him now or I'll find you in contempt!" Judge Whitehead said, getting agitated.

"But you're . . . . "

"Confound it man do as you're told, or I'll fine

you a dollar for every second that man is still in chains!" the judge shouted.

Squeaky had the shackles off in less time than it took to sneeze, then stood back with his hand on his revolver.

"Now what's this all about Roy?" the judge asked in a calm manner.

"Well Larry I was . . . ."

"This man's a killer your Hon . . . " the deputy started to say.

BANG! The judge's gavel hit the bench.

"Deputy Butts, gag yourself."

"What?" the deputy asked astonished.

"You heard me, gag yourself. This is my court and I'll say who talks and when, now gag yourself or pay a fifty dollar fine . . . NOW!"

The young deputy looked around desperately for a gag. Roy pulled off his sweaty bandanna and handed it to him. The lawman hesitated for a second, thought about losing two months wages and then gagged himself.

"Sorry for the disruption Roy, now please continue your story," the judge said, "without further interruption," as he looked stonily at the deputy.

Rogue River Roy told what had happened the day before and who had witnessed the shooting. He even included the deputy's entrance to the saloon and mentioned Ma's comments.

Judge Whitehead thought for a moment, then looked at Deputy Butts and said, "Do you know that the man you arrested saved Sheriff Smith's life? Do you further know that this man has collected the bounty on over half a dozen outlaws and is an honest, upright citizen. And while we're on the subject did you check for a bounty on Vermilion?"

"No your honor . . ." the deputy mumbled through his gag.

"Did you even know he had been killed?" the judge interrupted.

"Well I was go . . . ."

"You didn't even question any bystanders, did you?" quizzed the judge.

"I thought I . . . ."

"No you didn't think at *all* Squeaky. I don't know if I'm more amazed by your arrogance or your stupidity." The judge said, shaking his head.

"Now in the future when Roy tells you something is so, it is, unless he's telling you a tall tale. Now apologize, shake hands and let this be the end of it."

"But your Honor, this . . . . " Squeaky started to mumble through his gag, as Sheriff Pokey Smith came staggering through the door to the courtroom shouting, "Hold every thing! I just came to and Ma said you were gonn'a hang Roy for murder." He stood there with a glassy look in his eyes and a blood stained bandage around his head as he swayed unsteadily on his feet.

BANG! Went the gavel. "What is it with the lawmen in this town? You'd think it was their sworn duty to interrupt the proceedings of this court," Judge Whitehead said. "Now sit down Pokey, before you fall down. Are we still on for poker next Friday night, Roy?"

"Yes your Honor," Roy answered.

"Very well then, BANG! This court's adjourned."

*   *   *

Roy left the County Courthouse and headed straight for the blacksmith's shop. He found Mike Hammer hard at work making a set of mule shoes - rivulets of sweat running down his muscular arms. The old mule skinner stepped to the forge and took over pumping the bellows, with a nod to Mike.

When Hammer finished the last shoe in the set he looked up and asked Roy, "What can I do for you?"

Roy said, "I've got a PLAN."

Mike smiled; he had been involved in some of Roy's PLAN'S in the past and was eager to help.

The old timer explained what he needed and told him his intentions and then asked if he could suggest any improvements.

"Well I think I'd use a couple of pulleys and a little stove black to darken up that overhead boom. Why don't you stop over to Clicker's, maybe he has some suitable wire you can use." the blacksmith said smiling.

"Great," said Roy, "I'll get the eye-bolts screwed in and put the boom in place. I'll leave the ladder behind the shed. When I step out the backdoor I'm gonn'a fire my old Colt .44, that's to let you know we're coming."

As Roy left he looked back and saw Mike shaking with laughter as he started pounding out the *Black Hand.*

When Roy entered the telegraph office Old Clicker looked up and grinned. He was tall and thin with a ready smile.

"What can I do for you? Old Timer, send a wire to collect a little reward money?"

"No! No! Nothing like that, my Ancient Friend, it's just that I have a PLAN, Old Withering One," Roy returned.

"Now wait a minute Roy," Clicker interrupted, "Is this another one of your sneaky, rotten, foul, dirty, low down plans that you're famous for?"

"Kind'a . . . ."

"Well count me in. I could use a good laugh," Clicker said, with merriment in his eyes.

Clicker Morrison and Roy were the same age and had known one another for many years. They delighted in calling each other any name that denoted their mellowing years.

"Great! But what's this I hear about the deputy sheriff going to hang you?" Clicker said, "Couldn't they find an antique rope?"

"Judge Whitehead straightened that lunk-head lawman out, so don't worry your wrinkled little head about that half-witted excuse for a lawman. No! I'm here about something more important, Old Fossil," Roy said.

"I talked with the sheriff and he's not pleased with his new deputy, but he's Councilman Smother's nephew and he feels his hands are tied. I told him mine weren't and I'd take care of it."

The old mule skinner told Clicker his PLAN. "Mike said you might have some wire I could use."

"Ah' I've got just the thing," Clicker said, as he reached into a box of junk parts and pulled out an old burned out coil. "You can unwind this, you should get about a hundred feet of fine wire, I'm sure it would be long enough for your devious scheme. Now for the long wire, I can let you borrow a spool of transmission wire just roll it up and bring it back and no one will be the wiser, Old Timer."

You're repeating yourself, my Decrepit Companion," Roy laughed.

"Oops! I must be getting old," the telegraph operator said.

"If getting old causes a poor memory, then you must be . . . what did you say your name was?"

At that they both laughed.

Roy thanked him for the wire coil and headed to the Murphy place on Pistol River to meet his young nephew.

Chapter Four

GREAT UNCLE ROY

Matt was watching, not helping, Nate carry in wood for the cookstove, when he saw a string of mules coming down the dusty road.

Cat gave a squeal of delight as she spotted Uncle Roy and took off running towards the old bearded mule skinner. All the children in the Murphy household called him Uncle Roy. The little ones even thought he *was* their uncle.

Some of the younger children crowded around, asking if Roy had brought them anything. Mrs. Murphy came out on the front porch to see what all the fuss was about.

"Ye scalawags leave that poor man alone he's been through enough these last few days, without the likes of ye tormenting him." The smiling woman said. "Now get back to yer chores we'll all have a nice chat at supper . . . get along with ye now."

"Awh Ma!" A chorus of voices answered.

"Get! The bunch of ye or there'll be no apple pie for dessert." She said, peeling some dough from her floured hands. "Maybe Uncle Roy will tell one of his tall tales over pie and milk." She added.

"Oh! Yes . . . a story they shouted," as they reluctantly went back to their chores.

"Welcome, Roy . . . Com'on inside and have a cup of coffee. I'll have Shaun and Trevor put up yer mules, come on in and set a spell."

"Thank you Lisa Colleen. I could use a cup of your fine Irish coffee and a chair to rest my weary bones." He laughed.

"I'll send for yer nephew when we get settled so ye can meet him." Mrs. Murphy said. "He's out, *supposed* to be helping with the chores."

"Did you say *supposed* to be helping?" Roy asked.

"He's a little stand-offish and a little sullen, but maybe that's to be expected with all he's been through. Don't be hard on him Roy. I'm sure he'll come around."

"We'll see." Roy said.

As they walked to the back porch Lisa said, "Yer a hero Roy. Ye saved the sheriff and killed a dangerous outlaw."

"Nonsense I was just there and things happened. I didn't do anything out of the ordinary. Besides I've still got the third brother to worry about. He's a young hot head getting a big reputation back in Virginia City. Something to do with a big silver strike. Whip'em Willie keeps me posted about the going's on of the brothers - well I guess it's only the one now."

"Ye better be careful Roy ye never know when

he might take a notion to even the score." Mrs. Murphy said, with a worried look on her face.

They were seated at the large kitchen table when Matt entered through the back door. He stood on the threshold not quite sure what to do.

"Come on in and meet yer Great Uncle Roy young man, don't be shy he don't bite - often." She laughed.

Matt walked over to his uncle and stood there rubbing his hand, "I've got a sliver."

"Let's have a look see," Roy said, as he took the lad's hand in his and turned it over. "Sure enough it's a sliver, almost a 2x4 I'd say. I think were going to have to operate," he said, as he pulled out his old Bowie knife.

Matt's eyes grew large as he saw the size of the knife. He started to pull his hand back, but the old man's hand was like a steel trap. He looked with pleading eyes at the grizzled oldster and then he saw a twinkle in those pale blue eyes and he knew it was all in fun.

"All right, operate!" He said bravely.

"Well maybe we better use a more delicate instrument for a more delicate surgery." Roy said, as he slid his Bowie knife back in its scabbard and pulled a pocket knife out of his trousers. It was a well worn three blader. He opened the smallest blade that had been sharpened down to not much more than a toothpick.

Matt closed his eyes as the thin blade came close to his thumb.

"There the culprit is," Roy said, as he gave the sliver to the youngster,"Better go put it in the wood box - waste not, want not."

"I didn't feel a thing," the boy said, as he examined his thumb. "Oh!" Matt suddenly recalled, "Willie said to say howdy, I almost forgot. He was the stagecoach driver, do you know him?"

"Oh yes, Whip'em Willie and I go back a long way, Black Cloud and I saved his bacon one time, but that's a story for the campfire."

Shaun and Trevor came in the back door, taking off their gloves, "Anything else you want us to do, Mr. McCoy? We turned all the mules out after we unloaded them. By the way what's all that newspaper, chicken wire, sack of flour, paint cans and wire on those spools for?"

"Shaun! Mind yer manners. I'm sure if Roy wanted us to know he'd tell us." Mrs. Murphy said.

"Well, now that you brought it up, I have a PLAN," Roy said, as his eyes began to brighten.

The boys smiled with anticipation as they sat down at the table.

"Now first of all this is a secret plan and can't be given away, so none of the younger children can be in on it. You know how little ones can spill the beans. That's only if your mother will go along with this bit of mischief."

"Shucks Roy, I've never known ye to trick

anyone that didn't need trick'en. I'm shore what ever ye have in mind will be fine." Mother Murphy said.

"Good, then let's call in the twins and we'll make our plans . . . oh yes and include Nate, he's ten now and can keep a secret."

Rogue River Roy explained the PLAN to the children and sent them out to gather the items needed to build the illusion. They would meet in the barn; it would be the secret area away from little prying eyes. The girls brought in the large galvanized wash tub half filled with water and proceeded to tear some of the newspapers into strips. They would dip these into a bucket filled with a paste of flour and water.

The children wrapped the strips of sticky newspaper around and around the chicken wire form making a life-size papier-mâché Spanish Conquistador. The head was shaped over an oil lantern so the light would shine from its eyes. A wooden sword held in a raised arm gave a menacing look to the helmeted warrior. The other arm ended in a red stump to give realism to this phantom of the night.

When the Spaniard was dry he was hung from two wires and white-washed. Later he was painted to give the details, appropriate for a ghost.

The boys climbed a tall tree on the other side of the pasture and secured one end of the telegraph wire, after slipping two black pulleys on the end. A short length of wood painted black was attached between the pulleys as a spacer. The other end of the wire was fastened to a darkened pole bolted to the lambing shed, almost three hundred feet away.

Early the following morning Shaun and Trevor climbed the tree and attached the warrior to the pulleys then tied on a blackened rope that reached the ground. The whole contraption was concealed with branches, to wait patiently for its *grande* entrance.

*   *   *

The next day right before supper a lone rider came up the road riding an old nag harder than he should have. As he dismounted near the front porch he looked surprised to see Roy coming around the corner of the house with a towel drying his hands.

At that moment Mrs. Murphy came out the front door saying, "Step down Deputy, yer just in time for dinner."

Butts must have realized he should have waited to be invited to dismount, but he probably thought these were only sheep ranchers and Irish to boot.

"I've come about the cougar that's been bothering you Mam, the sheriff sent me. Look's like you need a real man to take care of your problem." He said, as he looked over at Roy.

"Well don't worry about that now come on in and have yerself some vittles," Mrs. Murphy replied, "Were almost ready to sit down."

"Better come this way to wash-up Butts." Roy informed him.

The deputy walked away from his well lathered horse without even looking back, on his way to the rear porch.

"Oh! Don't worry about your horse just leave

her, one of the boys will rub it down for you." Roy said, disgusted at the way some people treated poor, dumb animals.

There were wooden pegs driven into the wall to hold towels, gun belts and other things, above the wash stand. Butts took his own rig off and hung it alongside two others that were already there before he washed up.

With a scraping of chairs everyone was seating themselves at the table as the girls started to serve the meal. The deputy sat with his back to the door. Roy never sat with *his* back to a door, he wondered what kind of experience this lawman had. Black Cloud entered the kitchen quietly. He showed Roy six cartridges as he pocketed them and winked. *So the deputy carried a round under the hammer, not too bright.* Roy thought. *At least with the blanks now in his gun he wouldn't hurt anyone.*

Near the end of supper the children started asking for the story they were promised.

"As soon as ye clean your plates and the apple pie and milk are on the table that's the time for stories, if Mr. McCoy can be persuaded to part with one of his gems."

"Oh please! Uncle Roy," the children pleaded.

"As soon as your mother says it's all right I'll tell you about the biggest cougar in the whole world. It made 'Old Three Toes' look like a kitten," the old man said, as he looked at Deputy Butts.

When they were all settled down around the table, Roy started his tale.

"Now this one's called, Big Cat, Big Teeth."

"I've seen some mighty huge fish in my time and I've seen some hellacious big bears, but I ain't never seen the likes of the cougar I'm gonna to tell you about. I should have turned the mule train around right then, when I came upon those monstrous tracks.

I left Gold Beach early one morning with my four best mules, Ruby, Opal, Pearl and Emerald, every one . . . !

"Everyone a gem," all the children shouted in unison.

"Children!" Mrs. Murphy said, "Let the poor man tell his tale."

Black Cloud stifled a laugh.

Roy continued his story trying not to smile.

"The mules were loaded with some grub for an outfit of miners located far up the Rogue River. It was getting late in the day and a fine spring day it had been, pale new greenery everywhere. The trail was still a little damp under the overhanging fir trees. A recent shower had left some mud-puddles here and there. I casually noticed one puddle was shaped like a gigantic cat track. It was so big it must have been just a coincidence of course. Then I saw another . . . then another! They were real! The stirred up water was still swirling in them."

"I had my old Colt .44 in my hand; I didn't even remember drawing it."

Roy pantomimed drawing his revolver with his forefinger as the barrel.

"The hair on the back of my neck rose up like

the quills on a porcupine. I called for the mules to close up. This was a dangerous situation, to much cover for a cougar to hide in and spring on us."

"These were the biggest tracks I had ever seen. Why they were bigger than I could even imagine and that's *big*. They were more than a foot across . . . ! The cougar must weigh over eight hundred pounds if it weighed an ounce. This critter would have to be almost ten feet long, not including the tail . . . ! That would make it longer than this table," Roy said, as he pointed at each end of the table and glanced back and forth.

The children sat silently with their mouths open looking at the table from one end to the other.

"A mountain lion that big would have a whole mule for supper and me for dessert." Roy said, looking serious.

"Weren't you scared?" Nate asked.

"I didn't have time to get scared, 'cause with an ear-splitting scream the huge cat came leaping out of the brush and landed right on Emerald's pack driving her to her knees. Em had been carrying forty slabs of smoked bacon for the miners and that scent must have driven that big cat wild. He bit right through the canvas and didn't even touch the terrified mule. Slabs of bacon flew everywhere. The three other mules came roaring at me in total panic just a wild-eyed blur."

"To avoid being trampled to death, I dove for my life off the trail and rolled noggin over boots down the slope. When I stopped all I could hear was that mule braying with all her might. I scrambled back up the slope like a wild man only to discover I had lost my Colt revolver in the tumble. My Marlin rifle was on the lead mule's pack and Ruby was long gone up the trail."

"Emerald was trying to struggle to her feet, but the cat was just too big. I had to save her. I grabbed a large stick ran over and started beatin' the monster on the head. He was so engrossed in eating the bacon it took about five whacks to get his attention. Then he turned his massive head and screamed at me, as if that would be enough to scare me off."

"Well it was more than enough, but I was so darned scared I got mad. I picked up a bigger stick and really started to wail on his noggin."

"Then ten inch teeth flashed in a shaft of sunlight, it wasn't a smile. He turned with distinct irritation to look at the puny little creature that was interrupting his meal. I bonked him on the nose as he stared right at me. Then he really got angry. He took a swipe at me with those deadly claws and shredded the stick, knocking it flying from my hands. He leaped towards me just as the mule kicked out. She caught him on the side of the head. It hardly fazed him, but it was enough to cause him to miss me."

"It was then I realized I was in trouble. I knew I couldn't outrun him so I jumped behind a big fir tree, but he saw me and started after me."

"Now that tree was about eighteen feet around at the base and I started running around and around the tree as fast as I could with that ferocious cougar right on my tail. Actually, I was on his tail. I was running for all I was worth and so was he. His tail was about eight feet long and it kept getting in my face so I grabbed a'holt of it. I heard a yowel behind me or ahead of me. I didn't know which. Then we really started moving. My legs got tired and I couldn't keep up so I just started sliding along behind. Soon my boots began to smoke and my soles got hotter and hotter and thinner and thinner.

What a predicament if I let go the cat would have me and if I held on my feet would burn up."

"What did you do?" Nate asked, worry showing on his young face.

"Lucky for me one of those slabs of bacon was near the tree so I jumped on and went bouncing along slicker-n-slug snot around and around the tree behind the outraged cougar."

"The slab of bacon started to get a little warm after about a hundred times of circling that tree. It started to smoke a little, then it started to sizzle and it started to smell real good."

"Boy you talk about mixed emotions. I was scared, angry, hungry, tired and getting real dizzy."

"We must have been around that tree a thousand times when I thought I saw Black Cloud standing on the trail watching."

As I flashed by him, he said, "Roy I .... never seen .... anyone cook .... bacon like .... that before."

"The mountain lion's tail must have been stretching because he was catching up with me. He was snapping those huge teeth at my backside. The situation was *now* starting to get serious. I yelled at Black cloud as I came around each time, "Are you gonn'a .... do something .... or are you .... just gonn'a .... stand there?"

"Will you give .... me your secret .... biscuit recipe, Roy?" Cloud asked.

"Yes! .... Yes! ....Yes! .... anything .... just hurry!" I begged him.

"Then the giant cat stumbled . . . he ended up in a big heap with me on top."

"Black Cloud grabbed the bacon first and then gave me a hand up. I kept spinning and spinning around. He started to spin me in the opposite direction and soon I began to unwind. After about a half-hour everything began to slow down and I was getting back to normal or as normal as I could get."

"The first thing Black Cloud said was, "Looks like I saved your bacon again, Roy."

The children all looked toward Mr. Cloud, but he was gone! His chair was vacant. Even Deputy Butts looked befuddled.

"It's all right Cloud's out back getting ready to tell his own story." Roy told them. "Now let me finish my tale."

"As I sat there trying to gather my thoughts Black Cloud started to build a fire right there on the trail. I looked at him quizzically."

He said, "So you can show me how to make your famous biscuits."

"Are you going to hold me to that?" I asked him.

"I could have asked for your rifle and your Army Colt revolver as well. You got off easy Roy," He replied.

"What he stated was true I was lucky to be alive."

Then he said, "I was going to save you anyway Roy, 'cuz the bacon was starting to burn."

"What happened to the cougar?" Matt asked.

"In fact I asked that very same question, I said, "What did you do to that big cat, Black Cloud, cast one of your famous spells on him?"

"No . . . No . . . nothing like that he lost so much weight chasing you around that tree. His skin got loose, he tripped on it, fell and knocked himself out, poor kitty. With that the old Indian smiled and said, "Now let's have some bacon an' biscuits."

They all sat there finishing their apple pie and milk, thinking about the story Roy had just told.

Cat looked up and said, "What do you mean, 'one of his famous spells', is Black Cloud a witch?"

"No little darling, Black Cloud is a Shaman, it's a kind of witch-doctor or medicine man. I don't believe in that kind of hooey, but there *is* something special about him." Roy said.

"Men are warlocks, women are witches," Sheila said, she was the *reader* of the family.

"Now if everyone will put on their jackets we'll go out to the campfire Black Cloud has built and he will tell us a ghost story that will scare the bejebbers out of you."

"Ha." said the deputy, "It takes more than worn out old Indian to scare me."

Some of the children stole a glance at Roy smiling only with their eyes.

Roy led the way out the back door and retrieved his gun belt. As he stepped off the porch he drew his Colt and fired his signal shot into the darkness. "Darn scoundrel, I missed him!"

"What was it?" Deputy Butts asked, drawing his weapon.

"It's that old cougar that's been giving us trouble." Roy answered.

"You should have let me go out first old man. I'll bet I wouldn't have missed."

"No you probably would have shot yourself in the foot." Roy said, under his breath.

"What was that you said? Old timer," The deputy asked.

"I said, don't trip on that root," He replied, as he led the group to the campfire flickering across the field in the dark night.

As they all found places around the fire they noticed Black Cloud was naked, except for a loin cloth and his bear-claw necklace. He had war paint streaked across his face in a striking zigzag pattern. He held a small flat drum in one hand while the other beat out a slow tattoo as he chanted. "Hey-ya-ya-ya, hey-ya-ya-ya," his eyes closed as though in a deep trance.

The chanting stopped - all that could be heard was the crackling of the fire as the flames danced toward the moonless sky.

Then the ancient eyes snapped open. The children gasped, hardly able to comprehend this scary Indian was the quiet man that had just been at their supper table.

"This is sacred ground we sit on. Be careful of your thoughts." He warned them in a large voice. It was as startling as his changed looks. "Three hundred years ago on this night a great battle was fought right in this exact place. A fierce Spanish soldier, named Escobar-Cortez led his small army of Conquistadors in a battle against the Indians that lived on this river. During the heat of the battle a musket exploded and blew the Escobar's hand clean off."

"Oh! How terrible," Mrs. Murphy said.

"The Indians defeated the outnumbered Spaniards, but most of them managed to escape with their lives. After the fight a great Shaman of the Pistol River Indians, a name they adopted after the battle, found the severed hand and were burning it in a huge fire. The shaman's name was Firecrumb. He was very tall and skinny with a long nose, bald head and penetrating eyes. He was a dangerous enemy to have and a ferocious warrior. As he cremated the severed hand he put a curse on all the Spanish soldiers that had tried to steal their land and their gold.

A horrible scream ruptured the black night as Cortez came charging out of the darkness on his horse the reins in his teeth a sword in one hand and a bloody stump for the other. He was trying to retrieve his severed hand to give it a proper burial. The startled Indians scattered, except for the Shaman, he threw some black powder into the blaze. A blinding flash jumped out of the fire, it startled the horse and it bucked off his unsuspecting rider. Cortez fell right on a spear held by the medicine man . . . . As he was dying he tried to crawl to his severed hand.

The Spaniard lay dead with his arm outstretched towards his black hand.

"Hog wash," said the young deputy.

Then Black Cloud passed his hand over the fire and a blinding flash occurred.

One of the children screamed and pointed to the fire.

The ashes started to move and a black stick started to rise out of the fire. As it moved higher they could tell it was a finger.

Sheila screamed, "It's a hand! . . . . The Black Hand!!!

All the children were screaming as the hand, the Black Hand, rose higher out of the ashes.

Butts got to his feet, fear showing on his white face. He started backing away from the fire his jaw working, but not a sound came out.

Far across the field, high in the sky, a terrifying scream came from a form emerging out of the blackness. The sound of a galloping horse racing towards the fire grew louder and louder! The form took shape. It was Escobar-Cortez with a sword raised over his head, fiery eyes glowing in the night sky. Blood dripped from the severed hand in the ghostly glow.

The deputy drew his pistol and started shooting at the phantom charging out of the night sky. Six times he fired his revolver, but the ghost came closer and closer. His face was distorted with fear as he backed away; suddenly he threw his weapon on the ground. Deputy Butts turned and ran for his life into the darkness. A yelp! Was the last they heard of

'Squeaky' as he hit the barb-wire fence at the far end of the dark field. He was never seen in Curry County again.

Mike Hammer pulled the black hood off his head as he rode his dark horse into the fire light, still pulling the rope tied to the paper Spaniard above. "Howdy Mam," he said to Mrs. Murphy, "I sure hope you saved a piece of your famous apple pie for me and maybe a little coffee, it's not easy being a screaming ghost."

With that they all hooted and had a good laugh as they headed back to the ranch house.

"Mike could you lead the ex-deputy's horse back to Sheriff Smith's house, when you go back to town and tell him thanks?" Roy asked.

"I think he'll be the one thanking you," Mike responded as he picked up the hastily discarded revolver.

Chapter Five

HOLD FAST

After talking it over and settling on a fair amount for board and room, it was decided Matt was to spend the summer with his Uncle Roy on the trail and the winter living with the Murphy's. Matt liked the idea of staying in a house full of busy children and a boy his own age to play with. The school was just a hop, skip and a jump, down the Pistol River Road.

The youngster wasn't too sure about going on the trail with his Uncle Roy, who was stern and bossy, not kind like Mrs. Murphy. She was stern and bossy, but with a pretty smile.

Early the next morning the old timer and the young lad started off to Gold Beach with all eight mules. Some of the children came out to wave goodbye and Mrs. Murphy kissed Matt on the cheek and gave him a hug. It kind of embarrassed Matt, but made him feel good at the same time.

She said, "Ye take good care of yer uncle and don't let him get in trouble with any unruly outlaws."

What she was really saying was for Roy to be careful and keep an eye out for Victor Vermilion in case he took a notion to extract a little revenge.

Roy was to pick up some machinery parts from the docks at Gold beach and take them to a new mine up on one of the Rogue River's tributaries. He was also returning a spool of wire he had borrowed from the telegraph station. They would spend the night in town and get an early start.

Matt had heard from one of the Murphy kids the only reason they were to stay overnight in town was so Uncle Roy could play poker with some men he knew.

"Where's Black Cloud?" Matt asked his uncle after they had traveled a bit.

"It's Mr. Cloud to you boy until you're told different."

After walking in silence for awhile Roy said, "He went to see Dancing Flower and will join us in a few days."

Matt thought about it for a few minutes and then asked, "How will he find us . . . if we're on the trail in the wilderness?"

His uncle laughed and said, "That Indian can always find you. He seems to show up whenever you really need him or at meal time. He has a kind'a sense about those things."

"Is it because he's a Shaman - you know . . . a witch doctor?"

"Could be," Roy answered.

After walking a little farther Matt asked, "Who's Dancing Flower?"

"You sure ask a lot of questions youngster . . . but I guess you wouldn't know anything if you didn't. Dancing Flower is his friend and you don't need to know anymore than that."

They traveled about a half-hour and Roy asked, "Have you ever seen the Pacific Ocean, son?"

"No sir." Matt said, "But could I? I sure would like too," as he danced around, excitement in his voice.

"Well come along then and we'll walk the beach to town." Roy said, as he led his pack string off to the west towards the sound of the mighty Pacific Ocean.

The salty smell of low tide filled their nostrils as the beach wind tugged at their clothes. They traveled along on the hard sand near the waves that continuously washed the beach. The mules left a long string of tracks that stretched out behind them like a spotted snake. The upper beach was covered with driftwood and provided a place to stop and have a bit of lunch. As they sat on a log smoothed by sand and waves Matt asked, "Would it be all right if I took my shoes off and ran down to the water, sir?"

"Of course son, just remember never turn your back on the ocean."

"How come?" Matt asked, somewhat puzzled.

"Because you never know when a rogue wave is going to roll in. Waves are not always the same size, sometimes a really big one will be mixed up with the little ones. It will knock you cup over teakettle and suck you out to sea, before you know it."

Matt started down the beach toward the water with a little apprehension, but as soon as the first wave covered his feet he lost all fear and became a wild young boy. He ran and splashed through the tidal pools with reckless abandon. Matt seemed to shed his cantankerous behavior while he frolicked on the expansive beach. Then chased seagulls and draggled a long seaweed leaving marks in the smooth sand. Next he dammed a little brook trying to flow to the sea. He wished Nate and Cat were here to join in the fun, especially Cat.

A whistle and a gesture from his uncle put an end to his romp, but he vowed to return someday. He pulled a giant seaweed up to where his uncle was seated on a log and asked him if the mules would like to eat it.

"I'm afraid not Matt, they prefer their oats, but as long as you have it here I'll tell you something about your find. What you have there is a Giant Kelp, but that one is hardly more than a baby."

"The big ones get ten times that long.   Now look at the end that has all those long green ribbons attached to the air bulb that keeps it floating upright. You see the long tube? It narrows down to a little foot, called the *hold fast*. That's what keeps it in place. Notice that small rock that is stuck to the *hold fast*, well if it had been a bigger rock, this critter would still be out there on the bottom of the ocean growing. So it's very important to pick the right rock to attach yourself to. So you'll make it through life and not end up a derelict on the beach. To tell you the truth son, one of the best anchors you can pick is book learning."

With his lecture over Roy helped Matt on with his shoes and stockings. He noticed they weren't going to be suitable for walking the trails. He'd have to stop at Horn's Boots and Saddles. Maybe a stop at the local haberdashery also would be in order to outfit his new charge.

The old mule skinner lifted Matt up on Ruby's back when they came to where Meyers' Creek entered the ocean.

"No use getting your shoes wet if you don't have to - water is leather's worst enemy," the old man said matter-of-factly.

Matt rode the mule as it splashed though the stream. From his perch he looked out to sea. "Look! A boat," he shouted. "Isn't it beautiful?"

It was a three master under full sail, heading north up the coast. It was close enough to see the white waves breaking over the bows.

"That's a schooner son and she's heading for Gold Beach ... and yes, she is a beauty."

"How do you know it's heading for Gold Beach, Uncle Roy?" Matt asked.

"Cuz' it's in so close on this tack and ships don't normally sail close to dangerous headlands." Roy said. "To a ship the land is danger and the further away you are the better. You see that hill up the beach?"

Matt nodded yes.

"Well that's Cape Sebastian and when we get to the top of it you'll be able to see the schooner again and Gold Beach too."

They watched as the craft disappeared behind the headland, its sails bowed by the wind.

The steep trail wound its way up the backside of the hill over a thousand feet high. They traveled through a dense growth of shore pine and hemlock trees. A thick carpet of pine needles on the forest floor muffled the sound of the mules. A hush cloaked the eerie domain as they traveled the darkened path. It was like being in a huge temple. Soft shafts of light penetrated the forest canopy, giving a strange glow to man and beast. The wind didn't penetrate the thick trees so all was quiet and still.

After an hour of hiking they suddenly broke out of the shadows into the sunshine far above the restless Pacific. The vista was breath-taking. The trail followed the top of the cliff, a thousand feet above the roar of waves crashing against the rugged monolith. A brisk wind once again pulled at their clothing.

"Look! Look! Uncle Roy, there she is, she's heading for those big rocks! Can't she see them?"

"You just wait, in a few minutes she'll drop off to the east and catch the on-shore breeze right in to Gold Beach." Roy told him.

"I can't see Gold Beach Uncle Roy." Matt said, as he raised his hand to shield his eyes from the glare.

"Do you see that plume of brown water entering the blue Pacific?" Roy asked.

Matt nodded his head yes.

"Well that's where the Rogue River enters the ocean and Gold Beach is right under those smoke columns." Roy said, as he pulled a small brass looking glass from Ruby's pack. The old man extended the device adjusted it and handed it to Matt.

"Here see if this don't help. Brace your right elbow with your left hand to hold it steady . . . that's it." He instructed.

"I see it! I see it!" He shouted. Matt had never looked through a telescope before.

"That's the *Wave Dancer* piloted by Captain Mortenson He's the fellow that gave me this here glass. He should have some machine parts on board we're supposed to take up river."

"You know a boat captain?" Matt asked, somewhat amazed.

"I've known Capt. Jack for almost twenty years. I sailed to San Francisco twice on the *Dancer*" Roy said. "He's a good man and a heck of a sailor."

"Wow!" Matt exclaimed, "Can I meet him and see his boat?"

"Of course - he's proud of his boat and likes to show it off whenever he can. Just one thing, don't call it a boat, it's a sailing ship."

"What's the difference?" Matt asked.

"You can put a boat on a ship, but you can't put a ship on a boat and the *Wave Dancer* is a pretty good sized *boat*."

"What caused the brown water . . . I thought all the rivers out here were clean . . . or clear?"

"Well they are mostly, but there must have been a gully washer inland and maybe a landslide, that's mighty unusual for this time of year son."

"How far is it to town?" Matt asked.

"About six or seven miles and we'll be there in a little more than two hours if you can get your eye unglued from that lookin' glass."

Matt was having an exciting day. An ocean to play in, lots of sand, a sailing ship, he'd climbed a mountain and peered through a telescope. Now he was heading for a town with gold on the beach.

Chapter Six

A GLEAM OF REVENGE

The dual blast of the .45's, drove the farmer backward through the swinging doors of the Silver City Saloon. Surprise was frozen on his sunburned face. Five cards were still clutched in his callused hand, all spades.

He lay crumpled on the board walk - tried to raise his head . . . then fell back . . . dead.

A tall man, in a bright red shirt, strode out of the barroom two smoking revolvers in his hands. He stood over the body and spit a stream of tobacco juice in the dead man's face. "Damn sodbusters - If'n there's anything I hate worse than a

sod-buster - it's another sod-buster."

Victor Vermilion turned on his heel holstered his guns and reentered the saloon. The poker table, now vacant of gamblers, held scattered cards a pile of greenbacks and gold coins. Vic wiped the loot off the table into his hat and headed for the door. The onlookers tried to melt into the walls, not wanting to get in the killer's way.

After dumping his *winnings* into his saddlebag the outlaw untied his horse from the hitching rail. As he started to mount a voice called out, "Hold it right there, Mister."

The gunman continued to swing his right leg over as he drew his .45 and kept right on going over the horse. He fired his revolver from under the stallion's neck in the direction the voice. A glint from the sheriff's badge caught his eye as he pulled the trigger. His horse started to rear up only to be hit in the head by one of the lawman's bullets. As the beast went down Vic fired three quick shots hitting the sheriff twice in the chest. Sheriff Badger fired once more as he dropped to his knees and then fell forward as the life ran out of him. You were allowed only one mistake in a rough frontier town. The sheriff had just made his.

Victor rose from his fighting crouch and glanced up and down the dirt main street. There weren't any brave souls ready to stand against his lightning draw. After picking up his saddle bags he grabbed the reins of a wild-eyed mare at the end of the rail, He mounted in a fluid motion as he turned the horse out of town. He passed the bank at a gallop.

"No by thunder - I'm not leavin' this jerk water town in a mad rush with my tail between my legs," he said. Vermilion reined the horse to a sliding halt and hopped off. He kicked open the front door of the Silver City Bank with his boot and strode in, Colt .45's in his hands.

There was no one to be seen. As he walked around the counter he saw the teller and the banker cowering on the floor.

"Take the money . . . please don't shoot me, take the money and go . . . please," the shaking banker pleaded.

"Open the safe and be quick about it!" The outlaw demanded.

"I can't op . . ."

BANG! The Colt barked shooting the banker in the foot.

"Open it right now or I'll shoot your other foot you lying snake." Vic said, menacingly.

The banker squealed with pain, hobbled over to the safe and started to spin the dial.

Sweat beaded on his forehead as he fumbled nervously and tried the combination three times. Vic's gun poked him in the ribs all the while. At last the white haired banker swung the heavy door open revealing several neat stacks of gold coins and piles of greenbacks. Vermilion holstered his weapons, then shoved the banker roughly out of the way and started to stuff his shirt with the paper money. He filled his pockets with as much gold as they would hold and then spotted a row of silver bars in the back of the safe. "Get me one of them money bags and fill it with these here bars and be quick about it." He said to the teller.

"Yes sir! Yes sir!" The teller said, in an unsteady voice as he picked himself up off the floor and went to his cage to retrieve a white canvas bag. "Here sir," the man said, his eyes filled with terror.

"Don't hand it to me, fill it up with the silver bars and don't dawdle unless you think you can work faster with a hole in your foot."

The banker sat on the floor whimpering holding his bloody shoe.

"You lied to me." Vic looked down at the banker. "If it's one thing that riles me it's someone that lies to me." With that he drew his revolver and shot the unfortunate man in the other foot. "Now you've got a matched set, you see your luck's changing already." Vic laughed at his own black humor, turned and walked to the entrance of the bank.

He stood inside looking at all the windows and doorways across the street as he reloaded his revolvers. Quickly the outlaw popped his head out and looked up and down the street. You never knew when some citizen was going to take a pot shot at you as you were coming out of a freshly robbed bank.

He noticed a black stallion across the street in front of the hardware store with a carbine in a saddle scabbard. It looked like a better choice than the mare he had taken.

"All right you," as he pointed his weapon at the shaking teller, "pick up those money bags and lead the way across the street."

The hardware store was handy maybe it was time to *buy* a little ammo. There wasn't anyone at the counter in the store, no big surprise he smiled. He spotted the ammo case behind the counter, holstered his Colts and vaulted over gracefully. As he was looking through the boxes for the correct caliber he noticed a pair of high buckle shoes sticking out past the counter on the floor. They became lost in the folds of a white petticoat.

"Good-day Mam I'm helping myself to a few boxes of your ammunition, hope you don't mind," he said with a laugh.

"Take what you will, there's not much I can do to stop you."   A nervous voice replied.

Having been discovered the woman cautiously got to her feet. She looked at the robber and said, "I saw you go into the bank and when you kicked the door in I figured you weren't going to make a deposit." She stood watching him a look of poorly concealed defiance on her pretty face. "Did you kill the banker, Mister Stoutworth?

"Naw, I just shot him in the foot a little. I'd rather leave live people in my wake - dead men have no fear."

Vermilion laughed as he put the boxes of cartridges in a canvas bag and said, "Here's for your trouble Mam," As he placed a couple of gold coins on the counter. You're purdy spunky for a woman and I cotton to that. Maybe I'll drop by and see you when my business in Oregon is done.

The outlaw was out of the door on his horse and headed out of town before the bewildered shopkeeper could respond. A shudder went through her body as she thought how cruel and totally evil the gunman was . . . but quite handsome in a coarse sort of way.

As Vermilion left town he stopped at the telegraph office and shot the operator in the hand when he opened his window. Then he shot the telegraph key, the batteries and every piece of equipment that looked important. He fired until his weapon was empty then casually reloaded as he looked through the gun smoke at his handy work.

"That ought to slow things down a bit at least till I can get out of this part of the country." *It's a long way to the Oregon Territory,* he thought to himself with a hint of a smile on his face and the gleam of revenge in his cold, black eyes.

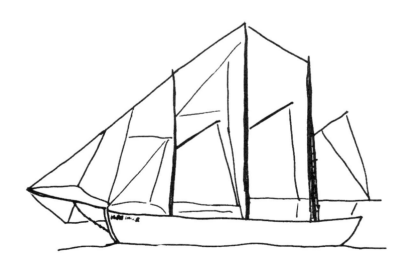

Chapter Seven

TENDER FOOT

Roy seldom rode his mules they were meant for packing and as long as he was able-bodied he preferred walking. That meant little Matt would walk too or as much as he was able. As they entered the town they could see the bare masts of the schooner rising above the warehouse down on the dock.

"Can we go see the *Wave Dancer* Uncle Roy? Please." Matt begged.

"Business first young man, let's get you outfitted; time for nonsense later."

There were rooms to let above the Green Lantern Saloon and Eatery with a livery out back. The stable man fed and watered the mules, then turned them loose in a large enclosure behind the barn.

Roy and Matt headed for the bootery located across the road from the hotel. When they entered the shop the odor of fresh leather and cobbler's wax filled the air. Matt breathed deep, liking the smell. There were saddles on stands, boots on shelves and harness gear hanging on the walls.

"Howdy, Stitch!" Roy said, to Mr. Horn who looked up from a boot he was working at on his last.

Mr. Horn was a short man with massive forearms and large hands that looked very strong. The top of his head was shiny bald with a black handlebar mustache under a broad nose. His friendly brown eyes had smile lines etched on each side. He wore a stained leather apron that covered him from his chest to his knees. He stood and extended his hand to Roy as he greeted them.

"Howdy yourself, Old Timer, how are those new boots working out?" He asked.

"Just fine except they don't go up hill as well as the pair you made for me ten years ago." Roy said.

"Well I can't guarantee the spring in your step, only what you're stepping in," the cobbler said, as he laughed. "What can I do for you on this fine day?"

"I'd like you to meet my great nephew Matt. He's out here from Missouri and needs a proper pair of boots to travel the trails with me."

"Howdy Matt, if you'll come around the counter I'll get a few measurements and we'll see what we can do."

Matt stood holding on to the work bench for balance as the shoemaker traced his foot on a piece of onion skin paper.

"Put all your weight on your right foot so the boot will fit well while you're hiking," Mr. Horn said, as he drew the outline.

"I see you've got a couple of blisters already, from today's walking, looks like you're still a tenderfoot." He looked up and saw a little hurt in the lad's eyes.

"It's probably those factory shoes you're wearing, they can't hold a candle to mine," he said, with pride in his voice. "I'm going to make these a little larger than a close fit. You're a growing boy and will fit into them in no time. You'll have to wear two pair of stockings at first, make sure one of them is wool, that's the best."

"Yes sir." Matt said, as he noticed the boot on the last the cobbler had been working on. It had a little pocket sewn on the outside of the boot with a flap that slipped under a strap.

"What's this for?" Matt asked.

"That's a knife pocket, son. You can put your folding knife in there and keep it handy. Not unlike the one your uncle has, but his is for a throwing knife of course."

It was news to Matt; he didn't even know his uncle had a throwing knife.

"What's this Mr. Horn?" Matt asked, as he pointed to a sticky glob with sturdy needles sticking out of it.

"Why that's a cobbler's hedge hog sonny . . . no just joshing you . . . it's a mixture of bee's wax and oil. It's used to ease those stout needles through thick leather and add a little water proofing." The tradesman said.

"Water is leather's worst enemy," Matt said seriously.

"Why that's true young man stay out of the water. You take good care of your boots and they will take good care of you. Come back around noon tomorrow and I'll have 'em ready for you." Stitch said, as they left his shop.

"Now we're off to Buck's Haberdashery to get you a proper outfit, one suitable for a mule skinner.

A mule skinner? I don't want to skin any mules, Matt thought.

"Come along boy we've got things to do before the sun sets." Roy said, hurrying the lad along the boardwalk.

A bell tinkled as they entered a cluttered dry-goods store. There was merchandise everywhere. Storm lanterns hanging on hooks from the ceiling, boxes wedged in the shelves, piles on counters, cluttered cases and barrels in the aisles, but no Mr. Bucks.

"Hello the store," Roy shouted, as he threaded his way through the maze of stock to the counter.

A muffled sound came from the back room. Soon a man emerged from behind a brown curtain covering the doorway. He took a large yellow napkin from around his neck and threw it back through the closing curtain.

Mr. Buck was the fattest man Matt had ever seen. He seemed to be swelling, ready to burst out of his clothes.

"Good day, good day, to all and what brings you gentlemen to my fine establishment?" The jolly proprietor asked, with a big smile crowding his round face.

"Howdy! Ben, this lad needs an outfit to do a little mule skinning up along the river. He's my grand nephew from back East away's and he has come to the territories to stay," Roy informed him.

"Well now sonny, so you're going to be a mule skinner?" Mr. Buck asked with his big smile as he looked down at his newest customer.

Matt stood dumbfounded. He didn't know about mules and didn't really know what to say. He just shrugged his shoulders.

"That looks like a pretty firm commitment to me." The big man said, with a laugh at his own humor. "Follow me back here. I think I have just your size in a pair of trousers." The owner said, as he led the way with surprising grace amongst the cluttered aisles. "They're not buckskin, like your uncle wears, but they're sturdy."

"I'm going to rent a room, send him down to the saloon when he's done Ben," Roy shouted. "I'll settle up with you later."

The bell tinkled and his uncle was gone. Matt felt a little uneasy at not having him near. *Then he worried... was that the same saloon where the shooting had taken place? Was Uncle Roy going to shoot someone else? Would the sheriff arrest him and put him back in jail? What would happen to me if my uncle went to jail again?*

"Don't you like the pants sonny?" Mr. Buck asked, interrupting Matt's thoughts.

"Oh! Yes sir! I was just thinking about something else." Matt said, dime novel images racing through his head.

"Now these will be a little large at first just roll 'em up a bit. Don't worry, you'll grow into 'em besides these are made from cotton canvas and will shrink. It's best to wash 'em first in hot water before you wear 'em, otherwise your legs will turn blue first time you get 'em wet." Mr. Buck told him.

Matt was hobbling along trying to follow the store owner and roll his new jeans up at the same time.

"Now for your shirt, one of these warm wool ones, like your uncle favors will do just fine."

The big man was already in another part of the store sorting through a stack of shirts.

"How about a red and black checkered one like your uncle wears?"

Matt shook his head . . . no, he didn't think he wanted to be like somebody that had been to jail and was so gruff and bossy most of the time.

"All right . . . here's a nice blue one," He said holding up the shirt. "It's a little large, but you'll grow into it."

Matt nodded his head yes and put on his new shirt and tucked it in.

He ended up with: a new tan felt hat, four pairs of stockings, two shirts and a belt suitable for hanging a hunting knife on. The jovial man tied most of his new caboodle along with the old in a package he wrapped expertly with twine and shoved across the counter to him saying, "There you go sonny."

"Thank you sir," Matt replied, as he picked up his parcel.

"Wait a moment, I better throw in something to boot or your Uncle Roy will scalp me . . . here take this red bandanna."

"How about making it two bandannas?" Matt asked, definitely not a slow learner.

The big man laughed out loud, "You're a chip off the old block that's for sure."

Mr. Buck picked a bright red and a blue kerchief off of a stack and slipped them under the strings on Matt's package. "There you go. The saloon is down the street to your right, you can't miss it . . . it's the one with the bright green swinging doors."

When Matt stepped outside the store he felt like he had shrunk. His stiff new jeans were rolled up and his shirt hung on him like he was a scarecrow. The only thing that fit was the hat and if he got a hair cut it would probably drop down over his ears. He thought, *I bet I look like a real buttledorf. I hope Cat doesn't see me looking like this.*

.   *   *   *

Matt stood outside the swinging doors of the Green Lantern Saloon trying to see through the crack. He was uncertain about entering, as he had never been inside a rowdy place like this before. Suddenly the doors swung outward and knocked him flat on his backside. He landed on the boardwalk, his package still clutched in his arms. A tall glassy-eyed man strode right over him and kept on walking like Matt wasn't even there.

Before he knew it there was a big woman helping him up and dusting him off.

"Goodness gracious child, never hang around swinging doors, the craziest people come through 'em and some of 'em are drunker'n a skunk."

She had picked him up and ushered him through the green doors before he knew what was happening.

"You must be Matt? Come on I'll take you to your uncle's table. He's over to the livery checking on his mules. He'll be back in a jiffy. You might as well have a little taste of pie and some milk while you're waiting. By the way, everyone calls me Ma. I'm a friend of Roy's. I was here the day he shot Vermilion, boy that was really something. He saved the sheriff's life, I saw it all. That uncle of yours is sure a cool one. Well me chattering ain't getting anything on the table."

With that she left Matt sitting at the table looking around the large room. Across the plank floor a few rough looking men were engaged in a card came. A bedraggled man was placing some freshly polished spittoons back where they belonged. Another man, with a neatly trimmed mustache, stood behind the bar. He had on a white shirt with the sleeves pushed up and wide black garters on each arm. He smiled at Matt when their eye's met, as he polished some glasses.

Ma was back at the table with a glass of milk and a slice of apple pie.

"Here you go sonny this should keep you busy till Roy shows up. Let me take that package and I'll put it here on this vacant chair."

At that moment the doors swung open, Ma looked up with a start and then relaxed. She quickly recognized a familiar silhouette, one she was a little sweet on.

Roy headed for the table. "Well Matt, it looks as if you've found my favorite place in town." Roy said, as he glanced down inadvertently at a dark bloodstain on the floor. A strange look washed over his normally calm face as he seemed to crumple into a chair. He suddenly looked old. He sat there silent.

"I heard what you did to Squeaky, Roy, served him right that sorry excuse for a law man." Ma said, trying to distract Roy from his thoughts.

"Can I get you anything Roy?" Ma asked.

Roy shook his head no then he noticed Matt's package on the other chair and smiled as he said, "It appears you got something to boot from Old Shylock . . . Mr. Buck to you son. He calls me 'The Old Skinflint.' It's all in fun. Well, finish up your milk and we'll go down to the docks and say howdy to Captain Mortenson."

*   *   *

The docks were cluttered with boxes, bags, barrels and stacks of goods, some of them being moved on hand trucks or trundle wagons. Stevedores and sailors were unloading the *Wave Dancer* as she tugged lightly at her mooring lines. An odor of tar and salt came off the sailing ship as the late afternoon sun warmed her decks.

"Be careful son. Stick real close to me so you

won't get under-foot." Roy told Matt. "Hello Captain Jack!" Roy bellowed.

He waited a minute and then shouted again.

"Why don't you go on the boat and find him Uncle Roy?" Matt asked.

"You always ask permission before you board a man's boat, even if it's a rowboat and remember this is a *sailing ship*. A ship is kind'a like a little country and the captain is the king. He's the law.

"Like the sheriff?" Matt asked.

"Somewhat." Roy responded.

"Hello you old scoundrel, come aboard, have a cup of coffee and we'll settle up." A big man in a white shirt and black dungarees called out.

He was wearing a cap with a short bill on it and the stub of a fat cigar was stuck in the corner of his mouth. His ruddy face was clean shaven except for red sideburns and a small mustache.

Captain Jack led the way aft to his cabin and offered Roy a chair. Then he turned to Matt and said, "And who might you be lad?"

"I'm Matt . . . your majesty."

Roy let out a laugh and the captain tried to suppress a smile.

"Call me Captain Jack, Matt and we'll get along just fine. "Well Matt, are you here looking for a job?"

Matt was surprised. He didn't expect such a question.

"Cuz if you are I already have a good cabin boy, but come around in a couple of years when he becomes a deckhand and we'll see."

There was a knock on the cabin door and a

boy, about twelve, entered carrying a tray with three cups, a pot and a little loaf of some kind of bread. He set it down on a large chart table stealing a glance at the captain's guests.

"Will that be all sir?" The lad asked.

The captain looked at Matt and inquired, "Would you like to take a look at the *Wave Dancer* son?"

"Oh yes sir, could I?" He replied excitedly. He glanced at his uncle who nodded yes.

"Tell the cook you're busy with the captain's business. Take this young gentleman on a tour of the ship, but stay out of the way of the stevedores. Be off with you now." Captain Jack ordered.

As the two boys left the cabin the captain looked over at Roy and asked, "Well . . . what do you think of him?"

"He's a little surly, but he'll work out just fine . . . ."

"What! . . . No, not Matt - my son the cabin boy," The captain interrupted.

"You mean that's little Morgan? I didn't recognize him. He was only about six the last time I saw him. I still pictured him as a little shaver."

"They seem to grow up faster than you want them to in some ways and not fast enough in others." The captain reflected as he poured coffee in their cups.

"He's the youngest and the last of 'em. My oldest has his own small schooner now, the *Anna* and is sailing between the South Coast and Portland. My middle boy is up in the Puget Sound first mate on one of the mosquito fleet."

How about your two girls," Roy asked.

"The oldest is married and the youngest is engaged. Makes me fell like I'm getting old, how are you doing Roy?"

"I've been livin' a pretty good life, doing what I want to do, when I want to do it." He looked around for a knife to cut the bread and finally pulled out his old Bowie knife and sliced off a chunk. It made the captain smile so he cut off one for him too.

"Now it looks like I'm saddled with an unasked for responsibility, but he's kin and I guess I'll do whatever I have to do to raise him proper."

In about an hour the two lads came back to the captain's cabin flushed with the exuberance of youth, trying to settle down before they were told to. The two old friends stood, shook hands, their business concluded.

"I'll pick up the supplies and machinery tomorrow morning on my way out of town Captain, so I'll see you then - unless you have another brass telescope you want to lose?" Roy said, with a suppressed grin.

"That's right - it's Friday, game night. Am I invited?"

"Of course Jack, you're always welcome. You don't have to ask. See you in the judge's chamber's about eight o'clock." Roy said, as he headed out the cabin door with Matt following closely.

Chapter Eight

FIRST NIGHT ON THE TRAIL

They slowly climbed the trail as it snaked its way inland, away from the mighty ocean. It didn't take long for Matt's little legs to tire. He struggled to keep up with the mule train, but it seemed his legs weren't quite long enough. The well worn path became a tunnel as the scrubby coastal pines and spruce gave way to the towering fir trees, hundreds of feet high.

The eight beasts of burden were loaded with mail, food, tools and machinery parts, destined for a mining operation far up the Rogue River.

Before leaving town they had stopped at the cobbler's to pick up Matt's new boots. He was thrilled when he spotted the little knife pocket sewn on the outside of his left boot, but disappointed when he found it empty. His new boots felt much better than his brogans, even though they were still stiff and hurt a little. Matt hoped they would camp soon. He was really getting tired, as he wasn't used to walking up and down the hills. Missouri was a pretty flat state and what he thought were mountains back there were only foothills out here.

Matt fell further and further behind. At last the tail end mule stopped and his uncle came walking back along the trail toward him.

"You're going to have to keep up son if you don't a cougar might just pick you off for a tidbit. Here give me your hat." Roy said. The lad did as requested and handed his uncle his new hat then looked nervously in the brush for a lurking mountain lion.

The old man took a little bottle out of his vest pocket, popped a cork out and extracted a single Lucifer. Next he found a few twigs and dry grass and then started a small fire in the middle of the trail. Evelyn the last mule moved up trail a little when she smelled the smoke and looked nervously back over her shoulder. After the fire burned a few minutes, Roy picked up a flaming twig and blew it out. Then using the blacked end drew a large pair of eyes on the back of Matt's tan hat.

"What's that for?" the curious lad asked.

"That will keep the cougars from attacking you. They will think you're looking at them and will be put off by it."

Matt looked skeptically at his uncle's art work and then placed the hat on his head. He noticed his uncle's dappled almost shapeless old hat had two large black buttons sewn on the back of it. *So that's what they were for,* he thought. Matt had intended to ask, but was a little intimidated to do so.

"Cougars are a little timid, but not cowardly. They'll attack a child sooner than take on an adult . .

and another thing, be sure to whistle or sing when you're walking behind a mule or a horse for that matter, so they won't get startled and kick out. But make sure you walk far enough behind so you don't get kicked in the teeth."

Roy then produced a short length of rope and tied one end of it to the pack on Evelyn's back and handed the other end to Matt.

"Here hold on to this, it will help you to keep up, but don't tie it to your wrist or make a loop in it."

"Why not?" the lad asked.

"If the mule gets spooked and runs away she'll drag you to death - that's why not." The old man said shortly.

"When are we going to eat?" Matt asked.

"When we stop for the night, as long as there's light we'll make use of it." Roy took his hat off and wiped his brow with a red bandanna and looked up at the sky. "That'll be in another two hours, think you can hold out till then?"

"Yes sir." Matt said, with flat enthusiasm, he was tired, hungry and his muscles ached.

"Here's a piece of jerky, gnaw on this and it'll keep you going till sundown," Roy said, as he pulled a chunk of dark, hard, leather looking stuff from the possibles bag he always carried.

The end mule started moving again, his uncle must have gotten back up front and started them off.

Matt tried to bite the disgusting looking meat and then threw it off in the brush.

Why do I have to do this anyway, I'd rather stay at the Murphy's, he thought. He started to think back, how he got here in the first place and it troubled him.

His mom's brother, Uncle Bartholomew and his wife Aunt Becky, decided to adopt his little sister after their mother and father died from the fever.

Alice May was three years old and cute as a button, with bright blue eyes, yellow banana curls and little cupid lips. Aunt Becky could hardly wait to get her hands on her. They didn't want Matt. They had three boys already. He felt they sent him out West to get rid of him.

He was bitter, having been orphaned so young and sent away by his own kin. He believed it just wasn't fair; it was as if life was picking on him. The boy was developing a chip on his shoulder a foot wide and the bitterness was starting to turn inward. The flames of rebellion were kindled in his young mind.

Hours later the mules stopped and he heard his uncle yell for him. When he reached the head of the pack train he found they had stopped in a mountain meadow above a small creek. The old mule skinner was already unloading the animals and turning them loose to graze on the nearby grass. There was an old fire pit surrounded by a ring of smoke blackened rocks and it would be the center of their camp.

"Gather some firewood and drop it near those stones." His uncle ordered. "Oh! And get some water too."

Matt found an old bottle and set it up on a log. Then he gathered some rocks from the creek and began throwing stones at his green glass target. With each toss his anger grew.

When his uncle returned to the campsite he looked around for the firewood and not finding any, yelled at Matt. "Didn't I tell you to gather some wood young man?"

"You're not my father and I don't have to mind you!" Matt said, as he went right on chucking rocks at his bottle in the fading light.   The old nimrod didn't say anything; he kept right on working setting up camp.

Along about supper time he fixed some bacon and eggs with a few biscuits to sop'em up. The smell of bacon cooking had Matt's stomach primed for a tasty meal. He grabbed a spare pie tin and stood near the fire as uncle scooped the vittles out of the frying pan. He didn't put any in the young lad's out-stretched tin; instead he scraped them all onto his own plate. Matt started to say something but was interrupted.

"If you don't work, you don't eat," was all Roy said, without even looking up as he calmly ate his meal.

Matt was angry and hurt *how can he treat me like this,* he thought, *I'm his own nephew.* It was a hard lesson to swallow and not very nourishing.

"I'll never do anything for you, you're a mean old man!" he retaliated.

"Think before you talk son." His uncle said, in his gruff voice still without looking up, as he sat on a log near the fire.

Matt's stomach churned and growled from hunger.

He thought awhile and figured if he was ever going to get anything to eat he had better humor the old man. Besides he was really hungry . . . he might starve before morning.

"What do you want me to do?" Matt asked him begrudgingly.

"Gather the firewood that you should have collected earlier," he ordered, "and another thing, don't break anymore bottles."

"Wh . . . ." Matt started to ask why, but thought better of it.

It was difficult finding the firewood in the fading light, but he managed to find enough to make a breakfast fire.

When Matt dropped the wood near the campfire his uncle looked up and said, "Don't forget the water."

"I can't get the water . . . it's too dark."

"It wasn't when I first asked you," Roy returned. "If you waited too long to fetch the water, that's your problem."

Even at his young age he realized it was useless to argue with this grumpy, stubborn, mean, old man.

As Matt was coming back from the little creek

carrying a bucket of water he stumbled on an old root that stuck out of the ground and fell head first into the darkness. He put his hand out to break his fall and wouldn't you know it, that's right where the bottom of that broken bottle had landed. Matt yelped then grabbed his cut hand and headed for the firelight. Uncle Roy was there in a flash. He holstered his six-gun as he gathered the youngster into his arms and rushed to the campfire.

Matt was amazed someone so old and wrinkled could move that fast. There was concern on Roy's face as he looked over the jagged cut and pressed his clean bandanna on the wound. He told Matt to hold it tight while he went for some water.

Matt already knew the old man always carried three bandannas, one to blow into, one to keep around his neck for sweat and one to have - just in case. This was his *just in case bandanna.*

*   *   *

"Here, put this stick between your teeth and chomp down on it, while I pull things together a bit with this thread." Roy said.

"Is it going to hurt?" Matt asked.

"Not me," his uncle replied . . . "oh you mean *you!* . . . well just a tad, believe me I've seen a lot worse."   Flashes of a dark war passed behind his eyes, scenes he had tried to wipe from the slate of his mind.

Matt placed the little willow branch between his teeth and tasted its bitter tang as his uncle tugged things together. He tried not to cry out or move his hand, but he flinched every time the needle passed through his skin. His uncle held his arm between his knees like a vice as he closed up the wound.

He stitched and dressed the cut as he must have done for many people, in many places, in many situations, calmly and with skill.

Matt cried out when Roy poured some smelly stuff on his wound, it really stung bad.

The child started to sob and it wasn't the pain from the injury, it was everything. He missed his mother, he missed the hugs and kisses . . . he knew he would never see her again. He hurt inside - that was the pain that caused his tears. He knew he was feeling sorry for himself, but he couldn't help it. A wave of grief washed over him as he let go of his sorrow. His frail body shook from the sobs.

*   *   *

The gruff old man held him tightly as a tear ran down his beard. He knew the pain his young charge felt. When he came home wounded from the war he was greeted by three graves, the graves of his wife and two young children, killed by marauders. That tragedy piled on top of the horrors he had recently witnessed on the field of battle was too much for him. Roy went a little crazy. After a drunken blur, hardly remembered, he headed west. In reality it was desertion. He was on convalescent leave and was supposed to return to his unit when able. Fortunately the war ended a few weeks later and he wasn't missed.

Devoid of feelings, his faith in mankind destroyed, it took years before he talked, really talked, to another person. As a tenderfoot he nearly died in the Bitterroot Mountains, but was rescued by a hard old mountain man who set him back on the path to a useful life. It was the greatest gift one man can give to another.

Now once again his life had changed, he had a young life to protect, with his own if need be.

It was a chance to pass on the skills and knowledge - time to repay a debt. The rough old man looked the forlorn lad in the eyes, as he fought back his own tears and said, "You'll be good as new in a day or two, now buck up and I'll fix you some bacon n' eggs."

*   *   *

Later on as Matt lay near the campfire all snug in his bed-roll, tummy full, he looked up at the Milkyway splashed across the black sky. He thought back how he always finagled something out of his mom, whenever he hurt himself or if there was a promise she had not kept.

"Can I have a little knife to go in my boot Uncle Roy . . . sir?

"Not on your life youngster . . . ! Now get to sleep. We have a long hard day ahead of us tomorrow."

*   *   *

Something was kicking the bottom of Matt's foot. "Ouch!" he cried out.

"Rise and shine boy we got work to do," a voice from the darkness said.

Moments later a match flared and as he rubbed the sleep from his eyes he saw his uncle squatted down, starting the breakfast fire. It took a moment to remember where he was, but the throb from his injured hand brought it all back.

"Shake a leg son or you'll go without breakfast." His uncle called out impatiently.

"It's cold," Matt said shivering as the damp pre-dawn air rushed about him when he threw back his bed roll. He found his clothes cold and his boots stiff as he struggled to put them on. When he sat up a twig snapped up hill a ways. He could barely see the outline of the mules munching the dew covered grass.

Matt held his cold hands out toward the fire as he watched his uncle cooking their breakfast. "What's for breakfast, Uncle Roy?"

"Oatmeal mush - something that will stick to your ribs till noon," his uncle replied.

"I don't like gruel," Matt told him, as he shook from the chill of the morning air.

"You'll like this or you'll go hungry," the old man said a little abruptly.

"Were your clothes a little damp this morning? Were your boots cold and stiff? Did you check them for critters before you put them on? Well did you?" Roy asked.

"My clothes were cold and damp . . . what kind of critters?"

"Scorpions boy, we got scorpions from Lobster Creek on and rattlesnakes too," the mule skinner told him. "Don't worry about it I checked them for you right after I checked mine.

"Thank you sir," the lad said meekly.

"Now tonight, knock the dirt off your boots and roll them up in your jacket, then put them inside your bedroll at the bottom. That will keep them warm, dry and supple."

Matt thought awhile then asked, "How come you didn't tell me last night?"

"Because one experience is worth a thousand words of caution . . . that's why.   You remember I told you not to break anymore bottles . . . do you know why? Do you think that cut hand of yours will ever let you forget?"

Matt sat while he rubbed his injured hand, thinking about what his uncle was telling him.

"Now I'm telling you to eat your mush . . . you'll have to start trusting me at sometime cause you got a heap to learn." And with that he handed the lad a bowl of mush.

"It's good!" Matt said, as he spooned a little of the hot concoction into his mouth.

"Take it from the side of the bowl - it's cooler there," his uncle advised him.

"It's got raisins in it!" the boy exclaimed, "and nuts and stuff."

"The raisins keep it from boiling over and also gives it a little sweetin'. The sunflower seeds and other grains are what keeps you going until high noon. One other thing . . . make sure the raisins don't have any legs on 'em."

Matt stopped in mid-swallow and then he saw that twinkle in his uncle's pale blue eyes and tried to smile around a mouthful of mush.

*   *   *

Matt's blistered feet were in no shape to walk another day and neither were his aching legs. Roy made a place to ride on Ruby's pack, between two barrels of flour and warned him of low branches he called sweepers.

"If you can't duck under 'em grab a holt of 'em and holler, HO! That way I can give you a hand if Ruby don't stop."

Roy saw the worried look on Matt's face and said, "Pay attention and you'll be all right."

Roy walked a little ways up-trail and hollered, "ROPE ONE," and the first four mules all lined up, Ruby, Opal, Pearl and Emerald, all in order. Then he hollered, ROPE TWO" and the last four mules lined up, Rose, Olive, Pansy and Evelyn. All were waiting to be strung together. Matt was amazed. It was like a circus act.

"How did you do that?"

"It's really quite simple if you think about it. Mules have a pecking order like chickens. All you have to do is wait till they sort themselves out and name them accordingly. Purdy simple huh?"

Matt liked riding at the head of the train. He could ask questions of his uncle and he didn't feel so lonely. It was really the beginning of his education. His uncle could talk from ṣun up till sundown, always be interesting and never repeat himself. Some times he would sing, his voice booming out seemed to warm the cool mornings. His favorite song was 'Danny Boy' even the mules seemed to like it. After the song they walked in silence, only the sound of the girls as they plodded along.

*   *   *

Roy was thinking about his younger brother Danny, killed in the Civil War. What a waste he thought. Noble ideas, youthful ignorance, ruthless politicians, equaled a deadly combination.

"How about a story, Uncle Roy," Matt asked. "Please sir." He pleaded as he recalled his uncle's reputation for telling tall tales.

Roy snapped out of his revere and mentally ran though his repertoire of stories and smiled as he thought of one the lad would enjoy.

"All right Matt, this one's called, 'Big Valley.'"

*   *   *

"I was up early and on the trail before dawn with my four pack mules. Ruby up front, Opal next, third in line was Pearl and last, but least was little Emerald, she was the smallest and bravest of the pack. We were headed back to town down the Rogue River Valley. Now when I say valley it's not what the flatland foreigners call a valley, just a slump in the ground with a brown mud-hole meandering through it. No sir! This is a rip roaring white-water, beat to a froth and honest to goodness ragin' river, with banks of solid rock a thousand feet high and jagged as a grizzly's yawn in spring."

"I could feel the warmth of the sun on my neck as it broke over the ridge behind me and saw my long shadow contrasted against the trail ahead. The trail was steep and narrow but the mules handled it with ease. The smell of evergreens wafted up the cliff from the trees far below. It was a great day to be alive."

"As I came around a bend in the trail, the sunlight reflected off of something brilliant, shining on the cliff below the trail ahead. Well this was to be investigated; maybe someone lost a polished knife or even a coin. I marked the spot by a small tree growing out of the cliff by the trail."

"When we got there I went down on all fours and peered over the edge. Darned if it didn't look like a pocket of 'GOLD!'"

"Some rain and a little slide had exposed a 'glory hole.' It was a patch of nuggets that had been deposited thousands of years ago."

"The shiny ore was a little out of reach, so with shaking hands I tied my ankles to that little fir tree across the trail. Then I lowered myself till the gold was within my grasp. My heart was pounding in my throat. It was because of the gold, not the hanging upside down by my ankles a thousand feet above the ragin' Rogue River. I began putting nuggets into my leather pouch. It's really hard to not get a little greedy when it's all there for the taking. I kept stuffing and stuffing soon I must'a had fifty pounds in my poke and started to pull myself up, when I heard a loud snap! I froze and started to untie the pouch, but I was too late the little tree broke in two and I felt myself falling towards the river - a thousand feet below. I could see three hundred foot tall trees that looked like sapling's, getting bigger as they rushed up to meet me."

"Now I've been in some tight places in my long life. I once had a grizzly bear rip the heel off my boot, a cougar on my back, I've been snake-bit, kicked, clawed, shot, stabbed, even had my hair mussed up once. Why I've seen floods, earthquakes, tornadoes, bandits, war and that was all before I was six years old."

"I was usually able to think my way out of any situation, but here I was falling a thousand feet to my sure death. Nothing could save me."

"My last thought was, *would my mules be all right?*'"

"Then a large shadow passed across me and giant talons gripped the little tree above. It was the biggest bald eagle I had ever seen. I knew in a flash those tall tales the old mule skinner told were true. Old "Halfway Jonah." had told stories of Big Valley, where everything was gigantic and no one believed him. 'Well I'll be.' I said."

"This eagle was more than thirty feet across with talons like boat anchors. He must've been out gathering branches for a nest and I figured that's where we were headed. Evidently the giant eagle didn't see me dangling below the tree. When he dropped off his nesting material I managed to scurry under the nest undetected."

"I waited quietly until he left for more branches.

Then climbed up into the nest and looked around, there were two gigantic white eggs warming in the morning sun. I put my ear against the shell and heard a thumping and scratching noise . . . I was about to have company! I had to do something real fast or I was going to be breakfast."

"I looked over the side. It seemed like a mile to the valley floor. What a predicament!"

"Several huge feathers were laying about the nest and I gathered the three biggest ones, pulled out my trusty Bowie knife and set to work. I cut the end off of one feather and hollowed it out, then inserted the other one in the hollowed end. It made kind of a wing. Then I twisted it till both faced up and started to cut a hole through both where they joined. Next I pushed the third through both feathers to make a tail. I used the piece of rope from my ankles to tie it all together."

"I really didn't have much choice as to whether I should jump off with this contraption or not. I was a goner if I stayed so I climbed up to the edge of the nest and launched myself into the morning breeze. When you know you have to do something, just go ahead and do it. The feeling of falling free, spinning like a maple seed, is not my idea of a good time. I must have fallen three hundred feet before I shifted my weight and found I had a little bit of control."

"As I was descending I saw a mosquito fly by with a grizzly bear impaled on his sticker. In the past I had heard the old timers tell tales of large mosquitoes, but this topped any I had ever heard of. He hovered around but must have figured I was too puny to be worth his trouble and flew off."

"I knew for sure if I landed in Big Valley it would be the end of me so I shifted my weight a little and managed to head south. The leather pouch of gold was still around my neck, I had forgotten all about it what with trying to stay alive and all. If I was going to glide out of there I was going to have to get rid of some weight. The gold had to go! I managed to save two nuggets the rest flashed in the sunlight as they fell to the earth far below."

"I was in familiar territory now and could see the trail I'd been traveling on, a green meadow appeared and there were my girls grazing away. I shifted a little and headed towards them as best I could. I was getting the *hang of this gliding* and thought I was pretty good. A sudden gust of wind blew me away from the meadow and I crashed into a stand of saplings. I had never been so happy to be on solid ground in all my life. I bent over to kiss Mother Earth and found out I had knocked out my two front teeth."

"I went to the dentist in Gold Beach when I got back to town, Dr. W. E. Pullum. Guess what it cost me? Yep, two gold nuggets to have a couple of teeth made. Well it wasn't all bad, having them two front teeth replaced with gold. They saved my life that very next spring, but that's another story."

The old timer looked up and smiled, a flash of gold lit up his mouth as he walked along leading the mules.

Chapter Nine

A DEBT REPAID

A cloud of dust enveloped the stage coach as it pulled to a stop in front of the Silver City Hotel. Whip'em Willie set the brake on his Concord and climbed down to open the door for the passengers. His guard, Shotgun Sam, threw down the baggage; it fell short of the sidewalk. The passengers emerged, a coating of road dust on everything and everybody.

"Right on time folks," the handsome Willie said, cheerfully as he helped his passengers down from their cramped quarters. The horses blew and shook their heads jingling their harness.

The weary travelers showed the strain of the journey and were in no mood for any jocularity. "The hotel is right this way folks," the driver said, light-heartedly as he picked up a couple of carpet bags and set them on the raised boardwalk.

Willie looked around for Sheriff Badger; he usually met every stage to check out who was coming into his jurisdiction. In almost every town Willie traveled through the local lawman normally met the stage. It was the place to head off any trouble before it got started.

He noticed a man with a large bandage on his hand sitting in a wooden chair, propped against the wall of the hotel. Then it dawned on him - it was the town telegraph operator.

"What happened to you Taps, trying to steal bait out of a bear trap?" Willie laughed.

"No sir! It was that damnedable Vermilion yahoo. He just stood there and shot my hand as I opened the window in the telegraph office, the ornery devil."

"Why in the world would he do that?" Willie asked.

"Cause he just shot the sheriff and robbed the First National Bank of Nevada, that's why." Taps shouted, as he started to get angry all over again. "He didn't want me to send out any warnings about him, the low down sidewinder."

"Did you say Vermilion?" Willie asked remembering the desperado Roy had tangled with.

"Yes I said Vermilion, there's nothing wrong with my lips, only my hand. Is there something wrong with your ears?" Taps said, getting riled up.

"No! No! Calm down Taps, I need some information for a friend of mine." Willie said, trying to mollify the excited man.

"Don't you, 'calm down' me," the injured man said, as his voice continued to rise.

Willie knew he wasn't getting anywhere with the wound up operator and decided to change trails. "Come on over to the Silver City Saloon and I'll buy you a drink." Willie offered.

The change was dramatic, Taps was all puffed up ready for a good argument, but the offer of a drink deflated him. He tipped his chair forward and started off toward the saloon without a word.

Willie shouted to Sam, "Water and feed the horses, I'll be back shortly." The look on Sam's face was far from happy. He was in a huff to say the least.

"Oh! And when you're done, why don't you join us in the saloon?"

The look on Shotgun Sam's face changed from sad to glad at once.

*   *   *

"Two whiskeys barkeep," Whip'em Willie hollered out, as he pulled two chairs away from a back table and sat down. He thought it best to wait till the drinks arrived before he started his questioning.

Taps grimaced then smacked his lips as he tossed back the shot of whiskey. "Ah! That's better." He said, as he settled back in his chair, "Now what is it you want to know?"

Willie slid his own glass in front of the operator as he held up two fingers to the bartender and nodded. "Now tell me what happened and start at the beginning."

"You don't have to tell me to start at the beginning, I know how to tell a story," Taps said, as he started to get rankled again.

The stage driver pushed his glass a little closer to Taps and nodded at it.

The telegraph man swigged down the whiskey and said, "Now where was I?"

"Can you tell me about the sheriff getting shot?" Willie asked gently.

"Well it started right here in this very room, over there at the card table. That murdererin', cardsharp, bank robbin', killin', disgustin' pile of horse cra ..."

"Vermilion?"

"Yes, who else? Now don't interrupt. Anyway he shot some hard rock farmer that was winning in a card game - killed the poor sod buster deader - than ah . . . ah . . . ah shot glass." Taps said, as he picked up the empty container and sat it upside down on the rough table.

Willie held up two fingers and said, "Go on."

"Well when he stepped outside Sheriff Badger confronted him and was shot for his trouble. In the heart, no less. Then he stole a horse 'cause the sheriff had shot his. That's another thing; he's a horse thief in fact a double horse thief. Then he had the gall to rob the bank. He shot the banker in both feet and he'll be laid up for a year. Mr. Stoutworth's running the bank from a chair with wheels on it now."

"Then he went to the hardware store and took a pile of ammunition. Next he paid me a visit and look what he done to me!" Taps said, as he held up his bandaged hand. "He shot up all the equipment and put me out of business. It'll take weeks to get everything operating again."

"Did he say anything?" Willie asked.

"Nope, only that he was getting out of this part

of the country, but you might check with Miss Hannah down at the hardware store . . . or maybe the banker Mr. Stoutworth."

"Where's the nearest operating telegraph station Taps?"

"Why it's over in Carson City, are you going there?"

"Yes, as soon as I talk to Miss Hannah and the banker."

"I'd like to go with you; I think I can pick up enough equipment to get me back in business. That is if you're coming back this way?"

At that moment Sam walked in after dusting off his hat on the doorjamb. He headed for the table where the two were talking.

Willie met him halfway to the door and handed him a few coins saying, "I've got to talk to a couple of people and when I get back we'll be leaving."

"But we have passengers at the hotel; we're not supposed to leave till morning." Sam said looking puzzled.

"I'll tell you all about it on our way to Carson City. Have your drink; get the horses replaced and the coach ready to go." Willie ordered, "I'll be back at the livery in about ten minutes."

*   *   *

HELP WANTED
Must be experienced with a shotgun.
Read – Write – Cipher
Dependable

A paper notice was tacked to the bank door - a new door - a rather stout new door. Willie read it as he pushed his way into the bank lobby.

"Mr. Stoutworth?" Willie inquired, as he approached a white haired gentleman sitting in a wheeled chair.

"Yes young man what can I do for you?" the old man asked.

Willie noticed a bulge under the folds of the blanket that covered the banker's lap. The two black eyes of a sawed-off shotgun peeked out. It looked like one robbery was enough to cause a little deterrent for the next robber unfortunate enough to pick on this bank.

"I'm the *'Far West'* stage driver and I'd like to ask you a couple of questions about the loss you had a week or two ago if I may?" Willie said, as he took his hat off and stood with it held in both hands in front of him.

"Oh yes, I recognize you now. I've watched you drive through town a few times pulling a cloud of dust behind you. Now what is it I can do for you . . . Mister . . .?"

"Ivers . . . Wellington Ivers," Willie said, "Did the bank robber say anything about where he was going?"

"If he did I most surely wouldn't remember. I was in so much pain all I can recall is how totally depraved he was. I still shake when I think about looking into those evil black eyes. I thought he was going to kill me. You could ask my teller, but he quit on me left on the next available stage heading back

East. He could hardly get out of town fast enough. Wanted to get back to civilization as he put it. I can't hardly blame him . . . what's a stage driver doing investigating a bank robbery, did he rob the stage too?"

"No sir, it has to do with a friend of mine. He was the man who captured one of the Vermilion brothers and shot and killed the other one in a shoot-out. If you know anything about that clan you know they're a nasty bunch and dead keen on revenge. I got a hunch your robber is headed out to Oregon to hunt down my friend." Willie informed him.

"I'll do anything I can to help catch that mad man. In fact I'm posting a hundred dollar . . . no make that a two hundred dollar reward." The banker said, as he looked down at his bandaged feet. "Why don't you try across the street at the Baxter Hardware Store? I understand Vermilion made a stop there before he left town. Good luck to you Mister Ivers and do be careful."

A rather attractive clerk greeted Willie as he entered the hardware store.

"Good afternoon sir, how may I help you?" she asked.

Willie looked around at the neatly stocked shelves for something to buy. He didn't want to appear he was here only to ask questions.

"I'll take a plug of that 'White Star' tobacco Mam," he said, as he continued to gaze around the store.

"Will there be anything else Mister?" She said, as she looked her handsome customer over and smiled.

"I heard you had some excitement here the other day."

"OH! My yes! A man shot Sheriff Badger and a poor unfortunate farmer, Mr. Parker, next he robbed the bank and shot old Mr. Stoutworth. The sheriff was a good man and very brave. I don't know how we will ever replace him. Mr. Parker had a wife and seven children what a tragedy. It will be a miracle if she manages to save the farm. The scoundrel came in here and bought some ammunition . . . some .45 long Colt. Then he shot-up the telegraph office and wounded poor Mister Tappet the operator. Shot him right in the hand, what a terrible thing to do."

"You say he *bought* some ammunition?"

"Why yes, he didn't even wait to take his change . . . he was in such a hurry." She shuddered thinking back. "I thought he was going to shoot me. I was so scared."

"You had a right to be frightened, you're fortunate he didn't kill you, those Vermilion's are a vile bunch." Willie said.

"Yes I guess I'm lucky to be alive."

"Did he happen to mention where he was headed, Miss?"

"Are you one of those darn Pinkerton men?" she asked.

"No Miss, I'm asking for a friend of mine." And with that he told her the whole story of Rogue River Roy and his dealings with the Vermilion brothers. He even threw in the narrative how Roy and Black Cloud had saved his life and now he felt obligated to repay that debt.

"Oregon!" she said, "he said he was going to Oregon . . . and he might come back." She reflected.

"Thank you Mam that really helps. Is this your store?" Willie asked.

"No it belongs to my father, Barnaby Baxter, he's not doing too well these days. The doctor told him to stay in bed and try to take it easy."

"I'm sorry to hear that Miss . . . err . . .

The young lady was impressed by the ruggedly handsome man and said I'm "Hannah Baxter, please call me Hannah."

"Well I've got to get going Miss Bax . . . err . . . Hannah," Willie said, stumbling over his own tongue as he awkwardly tried to say good bye. *She sure is pretty,* he thought.

Hannah reached across the counter and took Willie's callused hand in hers and placed his change there, "You'll have to come back and see us soon Mister . . ."

"Wellington Ivers, My friends call me Willie."

"I'll look forward to seeing you on your next trip Willie, be careful." Miss Baxter said, as she flashed him a beautiful smile.

The stage coach driver left with more than he had bargained for, his head swimming with the thoughts of an attractive woman and his duty to a friend.

He rousted Sam and Taps out of the Silver City Saloon and they headed out for Carson City to send a telegraph to warn his friend in Gold Beach. Willie hoped it would get there in time for Roy to be on the lookout for Vic Vermilion. As for himself he'd drive most of the night to make it to Carson City and get back to Silver City in time to pick up his passengers for tomorrow's journey and maybe, just maybe, buy another plug of tobacco, even if it was for Sam.

As they left the hotel Sam said, "They might sack you for taking the stage and using a spare team of horses to get back to Silver City. Did you think of that, Willie?"

"Sure Sam, but when someone saves your life, you're obligated to pay back the debt. Besides I was looking for a job when I found this one and I can find another."

*   *   *

Vic dismounted outside the Brass Rail Saloon and Card Parlor, dropped the reins of his tired horse over the hitching rail and walked the few steps to the batwing doors. He stood outside looking into the smoky, lantern lit room. He studied each face to see if there were any he knew in the boisterous crowd. The sheriff of Medford was not present. Vermilion smiled as he pushed his way into the dim room.

As he entered a few pairs of eyes looked his way. It was always the same in every town the only people to be leery of were the ones that looked up when a stranger entered.

He strode to the bar and ordered a drink and placed a gold coin on the counter. The saloon keeper seeing the coin said, "Are you interested in a little game of chance, stranger?" Without waiting for a reply he poured the whiskey and said, "There's a game going on in the back and they might have room for another player."

Without a word Vermilion picked up his glass and threaded his way through the crowd to the rear of the saloon.

Three men sat at a round table playing stud poker, one roughly dressed with callused hands and a tattoo of a whale on his forearm. The second man was older and he looked soft, dressed in worn clothes that had once been fashionable. The third man had the look of a sharpie about him and would bear watching.

The gunman looked down at the trio and asked, "Mind if I join you?"

"No, not at all," The older man said, "We could use some new blood."

The rough man smiled and said, "Four's better'n three, sit down."

The third man just nodded and kicked a chair away from the table with his foot.

They played for a few hours as the coarse looking fellow drank steadily from his bottle. The more he drank the looser his tongue became. Vic discovered he was a miner from the New Golden Egg Mine. Who had a falling out with his boss over some gold found in his boot. He was fired, but said he was too smart for them. He had already stashed a bag of gold out on the trail, just in case something like that happened. He roared with laughter as he told how he outwitted all of them. Then he became sad as he thought of the letters he would miss from his family back home in New Bedford. If Rogue River Roy got to the mine with the machinery and mail before he could intercept him, he'd probably never get to read them.

"What was that name you mentioned? . . . Mister." Vermilion asked, as he leaned forward in his chair.

"New Bedford, back in Massachusetts,
   it's where I'm from."

"I don't give a damn where you're from. What's the name of the man you mentioned?" Vic hissed, going a little snake-eyed.

"No need to get riled up, it was Roy, the mule skinner that does the hauling for the mine outfit. He's supposed to be there any day now with some machinery they ordered from San Francisco."

"How far is that from here?" The outlaw asked.

"About three . . . maybe four days ride." The miner said.

"Can you take me there? . . . I'll make it worth your while." Vermilion asked, trying to be less abrupt.

"I really don't want'a go anywhere's near there. I don't want'a face a miner's court. They'd probably hang me."

"I tell you what I'll do . . . I'll get your mail for you and give you a hundred dollars *gold* to boot how's that?"

"Pay now? - and I don't go near the mine?" The sobering miner asked.

Vic nodded his head yes.

"It's a deal, when do you want to go?"

"Right now," The gunman said. "There's a full moon and it's open country."

*   *   *

"Hey Indian! Ain't you a friend of Roy's . . . the one they call Rogue River?" The Gold Beach telegraph operator called out to Black Cloud as he passed the station on his way through town.

Puzzled the Indian stopped dead in his tracks and turned toward the waving operator.

As he approached the office Clicker reached under the window counter and pulled out a yellow telegram. "I received this yesterday," he said. "I can't give it to you . . . it's against company regulations, but it looks like information Roy should have."

"What does it say?" Black Cloud asked.

"I tell you what, I've got something to do in the back room and I'll just leave the 'gram' here," he said, as he placed a small paper weight on it to keep it from blowing out of the window. When he walked toward the back, he called over his shoulder, "You do know how to read, don't you?"

"You'd be surprised old man," Cloud said, under his breath as he nodded yes and said aloud, "U betchum."

When Clicker returned to the main room he noticed both the telegram and the Indian were gone. "Must'a blown away," he said, with a smile.

*   *   *

Black Cloud trotted all the way back to his camp south of town to pickup his Marlin rifle, possibles bag and tomahawk. As he dropped off his Army Colt, he told Dancing Flower to give him enough jerky for a week on the trail and after a quick check of his equipment and ammo he was gone in less than a minute.

He headed for the Green Lantern Saloon to talk to Ma and find out if she might know where Roy and Matt were headed. He went around to the back door off the kitchen, and there he found the feisty lady peeling potatoes for the evening meal.

"Howdy Mam, I've got a message for Roy and he's off delivering some goods to a mine upriver. Did he tell you where he was going exactly?"

A look of concern came over Ma's face as Cloud asked his question. She knew it must be very important for the Indian to head upriver to find him.

"Is it the last Vermilion?" she asked, as she dropped her paring knife and clutched her breast.

The Indian nodded his head.

"Oh Lord! I think he said, Grave's Creek and then up Coyote Creek - no that wasn't it."

"Was it Wolf Creek?" Black Cloud prompted her.

"Yes that's it; I knew it was some kind of critter."

"I know the area," he told her, "I best be heading out. Thank you Mam."

"Watch your back trail those Vermilion's are a mean bunch," the worried woman said, as Black Cloud left.

The Indian stopped at the sheriff's office to see if they had heard anything of Vermilion being in the area. He showed Sheriff Smith the telegram and Pokey said they would be on the lookout for the dangerous outlaw.

There was muddy water coming down the Rogue, Black Cloud noticed as he waited for the ferry to cross the swollen river. Must have been a storm inland to cause such a ruckus with the normally clear river, the old Indian speculated. Usually he would simply swim across but he couldn't take the risk of getting tangled up in a bunch of swift moving debris and ending up out to sea. His mission was important and he couldn't take any chances.

As Cloud left the ferry landing he set off at a trail devouring pace that he could keep up all day. He followed the north bank up the river. Cloud knew Roy usually took the north bank trail as he wouldn't have to try and cross the Illinois River at Agness. It was a large swift tributary that came in from the south. His friend would probably crossover above Illahe, around the Big Bend area, after that he'd just have to track him. As he trotted along many thoughts raced through his head. Would he be in time? How would he know Vic Vermilion?

The Indian traveled until the darkness closed in around him and he could no longer see the trail. The moon was only a crescent not giving enough light in the tunnel of trees to enable him to continue. He smelled some cedar and let his nose lead him to a tree with low sweeping branches. Using his tomahawk he cut enough branches to make a small bed of boughs. The Indian felt the rib side of the branches and placed them toward the earth, as his people had done for a thousand years. It was a cold camp, but that didn't matter. He fell asleep instantly with a piece of jerky in his mouth.

As the sun broke over the mountain Black Cloud was already jogging along the trail, he dropped down and drank deeply from a small creek he crossed. He rinsed and spit out the taste of stale jerky as he rose and continued his swift pace.

On the third day out just past Galice two sets of horse tracks joined the trail coming from the east just as the mule train had headed north. Cloud squatted and examined them closely. One of the horses made large prints must be a big mare or a stallion. The right hind track showed a bent nail. It would be easy to follow *if* it was the right horse. It made sense that it might be Vermilion. Not taking the animal to the blacksmith to have its shoes checked would fit in with the kind of man the outlaw must be. The second set of tracks skittered around a bit then started back towards Grants Pass. Cloud back tracked the new discovery for a bit. As he was about to turn around and retrace his steps to the cutoff he heard a horse whinny.

Cloud jacked a round into the chamber of his rifle and moved toward the sound cautiously. A dapple gray mare was standing over a form on the ground. It was a dead ·man dressed in coarse clothing, as he rolled him over he noticed a tattoo of a spouting whale on his arm. He'd been shot in the back. It very well could be the work of Vermilion. Probably happened a day or two ago. Looked like he'd been robbed, but who ever did it left his six shooter and horse. Hmm. Black Cloud didn't have time to bury the unfortunate man, but would if he came back this way. Right now he'd better get a move on. He thought about taking the horse but if someone found an Indian riding a dead man's horse they'd hang him before they asked a single question.

*   *   *

The horse tracks looked to be at least a day old and followed over the top of some washed out mule tracks. They appeared to be two or three days old.

It has to be Vermilion he thought. The only thing up this way was the hot springs -that's it! Roy's heading for the springs! I'll bet he is using the storm as an excuse to stop and relax in the warm, stinking water. It always smelled too bad for the old Indian, but it was one of the few luxuries his friend allowed himself.

A little before dawn the next day Cloud arrived at the springs, there was no one there. The fire pit was still warm; they must have just headed up trail. Cloud tracked the mystery horse and found where the rider had dismounted far from the springs. His boot prints led to a small hillock over looking the campground. He saw where the man had used the butt of his rifle to ease himself to the ground and had spied on his friend for a long time. Not finding any empty shell casings or any signs of a foul deed, Black Cloud was puzzled. He must have had Roy in his sights, why didn't he shoot?

Cloud pondered on the question as he tracked the horse now skirting the main trail not following the fresh mule tracks. Then it came to him - he wanted to capture his friend alive! That's why Vermilion didn't shoot. Any man foolish enough to try would have his hands full. Roy, whereas he always looked calm and easygoing was a very dangerous man. He was deadly with a rifle, six-shooter, knife and tomahawk. In a fight, he was a blur, emptying all his firearms he'd charge with blades flashing an awesome sight to behold.

Vermilion was being cautious; maybe he wasn't as dumb as his brothers. As Cloud studied the tracks it came to him, Vermillion's trying to get ahead of him! It's going to be an ambush! He'll wait till the rising sun is in Roy's eyes and draw down on him. It was just a few minutes to sunrise. Black Cloud took off on a dead run following the new tracks with reckless abandon.

Chapter Ten

AMBUSH

Bright blue, just as Mr. Buck said, Matt's legs were blue. The sudden storm had soaked him to the skin. Blue rivulets from his new jeans raced down the sides of old Ruby as they plodded along.

They had arrived at the hot springs in the late afternoon during a fierce rain storm, unusual for this time of year. Lightning flashed and thunder rumbled constantly in the distance, reverberating off the canyon walls. Matt helped his uncle rig up a rain fly between some pine trees and unloaded the nervous pack mules.

There was a mountain meadow a little ways uphill and Roy staked the animals in the middle of the lush green grass. They looked so sad and droopy with the rain bouncing off of them like little devil's pitchforks.

"Couldn't you tie them under the trees sir? There's a little grass and shelter there." Matt asked, as he stood with the pounding rain erasing the charcoal eyes from the back of his hat.

"No son, those tall trees are like lightning rods. One strike would kill the whole bunch of 'em. Then you'd have to load up all this gear and carry it down to the mines." Roy said, suppressing a smile.

Matt laughed at the thought of walking down the trail with a mountain of goods towering above him staggering back and forth.

"Now let's get in that pool of hot water and warm these old bones of mine," Roy said, as he headed off to the shallow cave that was the source of the springs.

Roy took his rifle with him along with his gun-belt all wrapped in a poncho and placed his hide-out gun on top. Matt carried a flour sack with some brown lye soap and a change of clothes.

Water dripped from the ceiling of the cave near the entrance as they ducked in out of the storm. It smelled like a hundred matches had been lit all at once and the pungent odor burned Matt's nose. Someone had hauled in a couple of peeled logs to sit on. Roy took off his boots and emptied his pockets then eased himself into the beckoning water with an audible sigh, clothes and all. He lay back against the warm rocks and closed his eyes. "Don't let me fall asleep, Matt. I'm just going to lay here a bit before I wash my duds."

Within seconds he was snoring. Matt thought he'd let him sleep a little and watch him so he wouldn't drown. The rain started to let up and before long the sun peeked through. The storm died as suddenly as it was born. Towering white, billowy clouds took the place of the black turbulent ones as everything began to steam under the afternoon sun.

Roy awoke with a start, "What was that?" he asked, as he tried to get his bearings. Then he noticed the bright sunny day outside the cave. "Well now that's more like it," he said, as he started to take off his clothes and began washing them with the brown soap.

They camped for two days and utilized the hot springs as the mules foraged. Matt was glad he had come along on this trip. He knew the chores he did were for the both of them now and not just something he was ordered to do. The feeling of being needed make him realize he was where he belonged. Somewhere between getting off the stagecoach and now he had gone from distrusting the old man to liking him.

Roy taught Matt how to make a fire using flint and steel. Matches cost three for a penny and that was way too much money to spend making a fire when you could start one for almost nothing.

"Now the secret is to keep the punk as close to the spark as possible," Roy instructed. "The further a spark jumps the cooler it gets and you gotta have a hot spark, especially on a cold damp day. So keep the punk, this piece of charred cloth, between your thumb and forefinger like this." The old mule skinner struck the flint to the hard steel, and a spark jumped to the black cloth and it started to smolder. He blew on it gently as he moved it to a little nest of tinder. "As soon as a flame jumps out of your tinder, move it to the fine kindling and in a jiffy you'll have a cracklin' fire. But remember have everything you need at hand before you strike your first spark. Now here you try it," Roy said, as he handed the boy the flint and steel.

Matt took the flint, steel and punk, held it as his uncle had shown him and struck sharply as he had been instructed. A spark jumped seemingly from nowhere. "Did you see that!" he shouted.

"That's fine boy, but what are you going to do with it? You made a mistake - what was it?" His uncle asked him.

Matt thought awhile and said, "I didn't have my tinder ready."

"And you weren't ready to blow. Now keep trying while I rustle up some grub."

As they sat in the firelight eating their evening meal, Roy looked over at the youngster and said, "Guess what? We have a new fire keeper . . . would you like to take a wild guess at who it is?"

 Matt smiled, he was getting used to his uncle now.

That night as Matt lay on his bed-roll he looked up to the star sprinkled sky and saw a shooting star streak across the void.

"Is a shooting star like a spark Uncle Roy?"

"Pretty much so." Roy answered.

"Then is it hotter when it starts its flash?"

"Yep and you can tell by its' color, white hot at the beginning and trailing off to orange at the tail . . . . I think you're gonna make it boy, now get to sleep were gonna get an early start tomorrow."

The next morning Matt kicked the fire together and soon had a flame cheering up the chilly morning.

After a quick breakfast they fed and watered

the mules and were on the trail when there was only a faint light in the eastern sky.

*   *   *

"Crows' *caw* and ravens *auk*, that's how you tell the difference," Roy told his young companion after he mistook a raven for a crow, as they walked along the trail. "Besides, ravens are a little bigger and usually travel in pairs unless they have a fledgling with them. Crows travel in a *murder*, that's what you call flock of . . . ."

"That's far enough!" A voice boomed out of the shadows as the sun broke over the canyon wall. "Go for your shootin' iron and I'll kill the boy."

Roy stopped abruptly and the mule shoved him ahead a pace.

Blinded by the low angle of the sun, Roy raised his hand to shade against the glare.

"Move one more time when I don't tell you to and I'll drop you like a puddle of cow plop, now with your left hand unbuckle your gun-belt and step away from the mule . . . real slow." The voice said.

Roy did as he was told then said, "All I've got is some machinery, flour and mail. Take what you want, just don't get trigger happy."

"I'll take what I want, where I want, when I want, even if it's your life . . . ain't no one to stop me . . . especially some wrinkled up old mule skinner."

"Who are you?" Roy asked, dreading the answer.

"Victor - Victor Vermilion that's who and if that don't make you shake in your boots you're stupider than I figured."

Matt gasped! He had heard the name in the Green Lantern Saloon.

"Boy!"

"Yes sir?"

"Slide down off'n that mule and walk towards me, nice and easy. If'n you run I'll shoot the old man."

*   *   *

Roy stood with his back against a tree, a single strand of rawhide around his neck pulling his head against the trunk. His wrists were tied behind his back. Matt lay hog tied at his feet, fear showing on his young face. The outlaw sat on a rock trying to fashion a hangman's noose out of a length of rope. He made several attempts and threw the rope down as he swore at his failure.

"I'm gonna hang your old carcass mister and while you're swinging with your face turning black, I'm gonna gut shoot ya. That way you'll die just like both of my brothers." The hatred flamed in his black cold eyes as he thought of his brothers, both killed due to this grizzled old man.

Unexpectedly Roy blurted out, "I tied the noose they used to hang your brother," he lied.

"Damn your hide." Victor roared at him.   He drew his revolver cocked the single action and took the slack out of the trigger as he drew a bead on Roy. Then his black face brightened, "You'll tie your own necktie too - that's it. You'll tie the noose that hangs you. Ha! Ha! Ha! What a joke that will be. Ha! Ha! Ha!"

"You'll never get me to tie my own hanging noose you'll have to shoot me first," Roy said angrily.

"Oh ya! I can make you do anything I want." The killer said, as he drew his razor sharp knife and placed it against Matt's slim throat causing a red mark to appear. "Now start tying or he starts dying," the outlaw said.

"OK! OK! Don't hurt the boy. I'll do what ever you want - anything, just don't hurt him."

"That's better." Vermilion said, as he used his knife to cut Roy's bonds.

Roy rubbed his wrists to get the blood flowing again and said, "Hand me the rope, I'll tie the noose."

Roy worked at his task for almost half an hour, winding the rope in a coil around its' self.

"Hurry up," Vic prodded him. "I don't have all day to waste hanging some worthless old has-been."

"Almost done," Roy said, as he pulled a loop from the coil he had made. "There that ought to do it," he told him, then threw the hangman's noose at the outlaw's feet.

Vic retied Roy's hands behind his back.

After three tries, Vermilion managed to toss the rope over a branch about thirteen feet off the ground. Then he led the stolen stallion under the swinging noose.

"Get on the horse. If you don't I'll cut the boy," his executioner ordered.

"I can't with my hands tied behind my back." Roy told him.

Vic grabbed the noose and placed it around Roy's neck then took up the slack until Roy was on tiptoes. He tied it off to a tree then cut the rope that tied the old man's wrists and said, "Now get on the damn horse."

Roy did as he was ordered. "Could you give me a few minutes with my nephew?" Roy asked.

"That's more than you gave my big brother but go ahead. I'm really enjoying this." He smiled, overjoyed that revenge was at hand - sweet, sweet revenge.

"Son it don't look like I'm gonna make it through this and there isn't time to teach you a lifetime of learning. If I had to put it all in a nutshell, I'd say have only friends you can count on and never disappoint them. Black Cloud is the best man I know, ask his advice in all things. Get as much book learnin' as you can. You can have all my books, I have a lot of them at the Murphy's and some stashed along the trails at Kooots, Ma's and the Widow Wilson's."

Matt started sobbing as he clung to Roy's leg, he didn't want to lose his uncle. He knew it was wrong to cry for himself, but he couldn't help it.

"Why does that mean man have to hang you?" the youngster said, as he discovered the throwing knife in his uncle's boot.

"That's enough blubbering and blabbing, get back boy there's a hanging gonna' happen," the brigand said, eagerly anticipating what he had planned for so long.

With tears trickling down his face Matt turned toward the killer as he pulled the knife from Roy's boot. Anger welled up inside the boy driving his fear away.

"I'll kill you - you dastard," he shouted, as he charged the tall villain with the knife held high above his head.

"No! No! Don't," Roy yelled.

"Ha! Ha! You're sure a feisty little one," Vic laughed, as he easily disarmed the boy and knocked him to the ground.

Roy sat on the skittish horse with the noose around his neck - helpless.

"I've got it, I'll slit the boy's throat, as you're swinging with your feet kicking in mid air and your face turning dark. You'll see the boy die as I gut shoot ya." The villain smiled gleefully, as he grabbed the child's hair, bent his head back and brought the sharp knife to his slender throat. Matt struggled vainly to free himself.

Bang! The sharp crack of a rifle rang out from the brush. The look of surprise faded quickly from Vermilion's face as the outlaw crumpled to the ground, dead. His black eyes open in a stony stare.

The excitable horse reared up and threw Roy from the saddle. Three more shots rang out in rapid succession, bark flew off the branch where the rope was tied, but the rope held.

Roy dropped to the ground as the noose came apart. Black Cloud raced forward to catch his friend by the legs, but he was already on the ground. Cloud stood there stunned, he expected his friend to be swinging in midair with the hemp collar choking the life out of him.

"What took you so long?" Roy chided him.

"I just got here! I was going to shoot, but he had placed the noose around your neck and I thought the horse would spook and hang you, but when he put the knife to Matt's throat I had no choice. I had to take my shot. What happened to the noose? Lucky for you it fell apart."

"Luck had nothing to do with it. Are you all right Matt?" Roy asked.

"Yes sir," he said, as he ran forward and hugged his uncle, tears of relief and happiness streaming down his face.

Chapter Eleven

A TALL TALE FOR THE MINERS

"How come you missed that hanging rope? It's not like you to miss an easy shot like that, Cloud," Roy asked his friend.

"I was kind'a in a hurry to get here, once I figured out what Vermilion was up to. I fell crossing that last creek and I didn't realize the front sight was knocked catty-wompas till I drew down on that hard-hearted outlaw. Looks like I'd better see that gun smith in Grants Pass if he doesn't charge too much."

"You might just as well take that Winchester carbine of Vermilion's, it looks like a good one, he sure won't need it where he's headed."

"In fact the horse, saddle, six-guns, the whole kit-n-caboodle belongs to you, as well as the reward. There must be a reward on a scoundrel like that."

When he searched the outlaw and his saddle bags they found a parcel of money. Some green backs, lots of gold coin, a canvas sack of silver bars, and a sack of raw gold.

"You'd think he'd be gambling and floozying around with all the money he had, but then revenge has a mighty strong pull." Roy said.

We got another day's journey to get to the mine, do you want to go with us or head out for Grants Pass now and we'll meet you there in a few days?"

"I better tie him across his horse and head to town now, summer isn't the time to be meandering around with a carcass. Besides there's a body back on the trail near the cutoff, I'm guessing it was the doings of that black hearted scoundrel." Black Cloud nodded towards Vermilion.

"What makes you think he did it," Roy asked.

"He was shot in the back, robbed and oh! He had a tattoo of a whale on his left forearm. I might as well tie him on his horse and take him along to Grants Pass too. Maybe somebody there will recognize him."

"If there's a bounty on this maverick, I'll have the horse shod and the rifle repaired, then see you there. I'll camp at my usual place north of town," Cloud told him.

The two old friends shook hands in the middle of the trail. Not a word passed between them. They just looked at each other, no words of thanks were necessary. Then as they parted Cloud turned back and said something quietly. Roy nodded then called for the mules to move out.

*   *   *

The trail got steeper and narrower as they climbed away from Wolf Creek heading for the mineral rich area where the mine was located. There were so many sweepers that Matt walked ahead of Roy so he wouldn't get knocked off Old Ruby.

"What did Mr. Cloud say to you when he left us back on the trail?" Matt asked.

"If he wanted you to know, he would have talked loud enough for you to hear." Roy answered, as he walked along.

Matt fell silent at the rebuke, mulling over what might have been said.

After about ten minutes of silence Roy finally said, "Well if you must know, he asked me if you could have his old rifle, if he gets it fixed."

"Oh! Could I? Uncle Roy! Please sir." Matt pleaded.

"You're gonna have to be careful with it and if I ever look down the barrel while you're handling it, I'll take it away from you quicker than a skunk can raise it's tail," his uncle said, looking stern.

"Oh! Thank you! Thank you!" Matt exclaimed as he danced around much as he had at the ocean beach.

"Don't thank me - it's Black Cloud that's giving it to you." Roy said, much amused by the boy's antics.

Matt was smiling as they walked into the miner's camp. The dreadful experience he had been through replaced with the thoughts of having his very own rifle.

*   *   *

It was late in the afternoon and the miners were about to quit work. The arrival of the mule train with their much needed supplies and mail, especially the mail, shut the operation down for the rest of the day. Roughly twelve men gathered around and helped unload the weary animals. When they were all unloaded, Roy told Matt to feed bag the lot of them and lead 'em up past the mine tailings to a little box cannon and turn 'em loose.

The mine foreman was an old friend of Roy's and invited him into his tent for a drink. Mr. Burrows knew Roy didn't use spirits, but was looking for an excuse to step inside and have his daily imbibement.

The cook stuck his head in through the tent flap and asked if Roy and the young fellow would be staying for supper, as he did so, he glanced at his boss for approval. He had been out of bacon and short of flour so he was quite happy with the arrival of his new supplies.

"Of course Baldy, I've been looking forward to it for the last twenty miles and you're lucky I brought you anything at all." Roy said, with mock anger in his voice.

A look of puzzlement appeared on both Baldy and Mr. Burrow's faces, "What do ya mean Roy, are you heated up about something?" The boss man asked.

"No, it's just that I got hung a little and Matt almost got his throat slit." Roy said, with a big smile.

"Throat cut!" They both said in unison.

"Take a look at the mark on the boy's throat that will tell the tale." The mule skinner told them.

"How can you get hung, *a little*? Baldy asked.

"I'll tell the whole story over supper you did make an apple pie, didn't you? This story is worth an apple pie." Roy gave a look that meant no pie, no story.

"OK! OK! I've got something's to do," Baldy said, as he withdrew his polished head from the tent and set about his chores.

*   *   *

The meal was served in a large sun bleached tent on several rough hewn tables. Rugged looking men in rock dusted clothes surrounded the tables sitting on split log benches. They looked as flinty as the rock they toiled at every day.

All through the evening meal Roy told of the heroic actions of Matt and his good friend Black Cloud. He built up their parts and diminished his own because that was the kind of man he was. When dessert was served (apple pie) at the end of the meal, Baldy asked if he wouldn't part with one of his tall tales.

Roy sat there a minute, enjoying the last bite of his pie then said, "I think I have just the story. It's about . . . ."

"Wait a minute," one of the miners interrupted, "How did the noose come undone, this sounds like one of the fibs you're always telling."

"It's true," Matt exclaimed, surprised at his own voice, it was the first time he had spoken during the meal. All eyes looked towards him. Aware he was the focus of everyone's attention, Matt was suddenly uncomfortable.

"I tied the hangman's noose myself." Roy said, in a quieter voice.

"Hogwash," one of the miners said, "How could you get Vermilion to let you tie your own noose?"

"You ever heard of Brer Rabbit and the brier patch?" Roy asked.

A few of the miners nodded yes and one of them said his pappy used to tell him Uncle Remus Tales, when he was a child. (It was hard to realize that this huge, rugged miner was ever a child.)

"I started off by telling the outlaw a lie."

"That must have been easy for you Roy," Baldy said, as everyone laughed, including Roy.

"I told him I tied the noose that hung his brother which of course I didn't. I wasn't even in town. He got so mad I thought he was going to shoot me right then and there. But instead he got the bright idea he could *force* me to tie my own noose. Well reluctantly I did and you know the rest of the story."

Matt wasn't aware that his uncle had pulled the trick on the outlaw and thought, *I better start watching my uncle a little closer.*

Roy waited until everyone quieted down and had charged their coffee mugs with fresh coffee then he started his tale.

"Now, the story I had in mind is about a little mining operation that took place not to far from here, a few years ago . . . ." Roy began, as he slid into his story telling voice. This one is called Heavenly Hotcakes.

"I'm not one to brag, but when something is good, I mean really good and you want to share it, you have to tell how good it is. Well I'd been making hotcakes on the trail for over thirty years and I finally stumbled on a recipe that made 'em so light and fluffy they started to float right out of the pan."

A few groans from his audience.

"That's right as soon as I flipped 'em they started off for the heavens. Now there are always drawbacks to every discovery. I could only cook one at a time, as I didn't weigh enough to hold more than one down."

More groans!

"To be perfectly truthful, the recipe or at least half of it came from Ma, down at the Green Lantern Eatery in Gold Beach. A mighty fine cook and a very independent lady."

"As usual, I'm getting ahead of myself; let me tell it as it happened."

"My pardner Engine Joe and I were hauling supplies and a little mail up the Rogue River. There was a group of miners that struck it rich up past Big Bend and they needed food and equipment badly."

"It was the first morning on the trail with eight heavily loaded mules. I was up early to fix breakfast. The sun was about to break over the jagged hills that corralled the Rogue River on its way to the sea."

"The cooking fire felt good against the morning chill. That's when I made the great discovery. I could hardly contain myself. I yelled at Joe to shake off them blankets and get over here and have some of the lightest hotcakes in the world. No kidding! I have to hold em down," I told him.

Sleepy eyed Joe said, "I've always had a hard time keeping your hotcakes down, Roy."

Laughter burst from the burly miners.

"No! No! I mean these are 'really' hard to keep down." I said.

Engine Joe grimaced and said, "And what I'm telling *you* is they're *'really'* hard to keep down. You make the best biscuits I ever ate and the best oatmeal mush, but your hotcakes are grim." Joe replied.

"OK watch this," I said, as I flipped another hotcake and when it started to rise from the skillet, I just let it go. It went straight up in the still air of the morning reflecting the rising sun. As the griddle cake rose to about a hundred feet, I drew my Army Colt .44 and fired. With a puff, the hot-cake deflated, did a few loops and swoops, then fell back to earth, much like a feather."

"Well I'll be," Joe exclaimed, now fully awake, "Do that again."

"We had so much fun shooting hotcakes we ran out of batter. I mixed up a double batch and Engine Joe sat down on a pack to eat."

"Now let me tell you about Joe, they called him 'Engine' cause he was as strong as the steam engine on the Rogue River Queen. He could work all day 'balls out'. That meant at 'full throttle.' (The governor on a steam engine used the centrifugal force of spinning balls to close the steam valve and keep it from running away and when they were spinning fast, the balls were as far out as they could go. That's were the expression, 'balls out' came from.) His real name was Joseph J. Washington, he was six foot, six inches tall, weighed well over three hundred pounds and as black as the smoke coming out of the Queen's stacks. He was a man to stay on the good side of and a man to fear in a fight. We went back a long ways, all the way back to Missouri as boys, before the civil war, now back to my story."

"Well it seemed that Joe couldn't get enough of those Heavenly Hotcakes, he ate until I thought he'd burst. Then the strangest thing happened, he started to rise up in the air! He shouted for me to do something! I was flabbergasted, I bent a sapling over so he could reach it and it held for a minute and then snapped off! I whipped out my lariat and caught Joe around the ankle and tied him to a large fir tree. He kept yelling, "Do something! Do something!""

"If he wasn't a sight floating like a hot-air balloon tied to that tree by a rope around his foot. Why he'd be a big hit in the Fourth of July parade in Gold Beach. I thought I'd have some fun with him. I said, "Do you want me to shoot ya?" I had visions of Joe looping and swooping around in the air."

"No! No! Just get me down! . . . Darn your hide, quit fooling around and get me down!"

"I hadn't seen Joe that riled-up in a coons age. Well I thought about it for awhile, and said, "I got an idea.""

"He sure did look funny bobbing around in the wind at the end of a rope. I couldn't resist, "Is this the first time you been strung up big fella?" Then I hooted and slapped my leg and doubled up with laughter. The roar of his Walker .44 wiped the grin off my face, as the recoil wrapped him halfway round the tree. I said, "Hold on Joe, let me get some of the girls.""

"The only way I could figure to keep him on

the ground was to have him carry one of the mules. Well one mule wouldn't do it, so he had to pick up two of 'em to keep himself down. If that wasn't a sight, him walking into the miner's camp carrying two mules loaded down with equipment. The miners all stood there with their mouths wide open, frozen in position. I had to go around shutting their traps so they could start talking again. Joe set one of the mules down and he seemed like he was going to stay on the ground so he put the other one down and found out he was back to normal, or as normal as he was normally, which wasn't normally that normal."

"We unloaded all the animals and passed out the goods, but the miners still stood there thunderstruck. They weren't going to let us leave without an explanation. It was then I told my first lie ever. . . ."

The miners sitting around the tables all scoffed about the first lie ever.

"To protect my new recipe of course I told them the mules were so heavily loaded that Joe had to carry them the last few feet into camp, actually it was more like twenty-two miles."

"Those miners were still a little suspicious and didn't quite believe what they had seen, but it didn't stop them from having a *hootdown* celebration. Those miners would party at the pop of a cork and furnish the bottle it popped out of."

The miners knowingly winked and smiled at one another. Hard men partied hard.

"The subject of our payment came up and they paid us off in gold. They had a great big box loaded with the shiny stuff that must have weighed twelve hundred pounds. I asked them if they weren't afraid someone would rob them of their hard worked for treasure.

"Heck no," the leader replied, "It's so heavy no one can lift it."

"I really hate to butt into a man's business, but these gents were asking for trouble. That much gold was like a magnet to every desperado in this neck of the woods. It could get them all killed and anybody else that happened to be there."

"Did you ever hear of Yellow Dog, Bully Boggs, Larry Loud, Vance Vermilion or Marvin Meanest? I asked the leader. Or the Waymen Brothers? Any one of them would slit your throat for the fun of it. They're the worst bunch of killers that ever slapped leather. They'll dry gulch ya, back shoot ya, torture ya and burn ya alive and that's not even the bad stuff they do to ya."

"Tell you, what I'll do. Joe and I will transport this here gold to the Bank of Oregon in Grants Pass and deposit it there for a fee of only five percent."

"Now the banker is a friend of my father's, from Missouri and can be trusted. His name is Irwin B. Upright and is as honest as they come."

"After talking it over with the rest of the miners they decided to let us take the gold and deposit it in the bank for the agreed upon charge as long as we guaranteed the safe arrival. We shook hands on the agreement. That was all we needed to seal the bargain. The only other thing was they wanted to melt all the gold down to one big nugget, to make it real hard for any bandit to walk away with it all."

"Well it took about two days for them galoots to get all that gold melted down and when they were done they had a block of gold about one foot square. As I requested they stuck a couple mule shoes in the top of the gold block just as it hardened up."

"Someone popped a cork and they had another *hootdown* to celebrate the making of the big nugget."

"Early the next morning I was up at the crack of dawn mixing up a batch of my heavenly hotcakes. The miners were still sleeping off last night's cork-pop'n and only a couple stirred as I called Engine Joe for a breakfast of lighter than air fare."

"We took a couple of feed bags and tied them with short ropes to the mule shoes stuck in the gold and as I turned the hot-cakes, Joe slipped them into the bags one at a time. As unbelievable as it seems it only took six hotcakes on each side to *float the gold*, but then they were big hotcakes. We tethered the gold to a tree while we continued our preparations to get underway."

"I yelled R. O. P. E. and Ruby, Opal, Pearl and Emerald came a running, all lined up in order eager to be on the trail again. Then I Yelled R. O. P. E. two and Rose, Olive, Pansy and Evelyn, came walking slowly out of the woods, not to eager to be second team. I gave 'em all a little piece of hotcake, to lighten their spirits, as we hit the trail for Grants Pass."

"Engine Joe picked up the big nugget, actually he was holding it down and headed up the trail with long buoyant steps. A groggy, sleepy eyed miner looked up from his bedroll, saw Joe disappear around a bend, kind'a floating up the trail carrying the big block of gold, then lay back down. He popped up a second later with a look of disbelief on his face, shook his head and fell back to sleep."

"Well now that much gold in one place is going to be like a carcass on the desert attracting buzzards. Gold news travels fast amongst bad people."

"I didn't like the idea of Engine Joe carrying that gold, without his gun-hand free, he was an easy target. We tied the gold securely above Rose as she was in the middle of the pack string and the most sure-footed of the mules."

*   *   *

"It was a surprise, but not entirely unexpected, when a couple of shots rang out. A big voice boomed out right after them."

"Stick-Em-Up . . . ! Or I'll drop you where you stand!"

"I recognized the 'voice,' there was only one voice that loud and cruel, it was Larry Loud. He had the loudest voice in the world, even when he whispered, it hurt your ears. He was not only loud he was mean to boot, I mean really mean, mean."

"I saw him shoot a man, back a few years ago, in Langlois, for taking the last piece of blackberry pie at the Greasy Spoon Cafe. He was out of town before the sheriff knew what happened. The posse tried to cut his trail, but he disappeared without a trace, this was the first I'd heard of him since then."

"Throw down your shootin' irons and be quick or be dead!" the booming voice said."

"I still couldn't see him with all the brush along the trail, but I'd bet he could see me. I unbuckled my gun belt and let it slip to ground."

"I said, drop it, fool!"

"So he couldn't see me, he was talking at Joe. I scooped up my gun belt and headed back down the trail as quietly as I could. My plan was to circle around and get the drop on him from behind."

"Then the tremendous voice said, "Where's the gold big fella? Don't give me any trouble and you'll live to see another sunrise.""

"I heard Engine Joe say, "Why it's on Rose, the fifth mule back, I'll call her up here.""

"I'll bet he has a plan, I mused."
And with that he gave a whistle and said, "Rose, Rose, c'mon gal."

"Rose moved past the other mules on the side of the trail making quite a bit of noise crashing through the brush. I used the noise to cover my own sounds as I moved into position."

"Purdy smart, using a noise to cover a noise." One of the miners said."

"Then I saw him, it *was* Larry Loud and he had a sawed-off shotgun aimed at Joe's middle."

"You never go up against a shotgun with a hand gun, *I better wait and see what happens*, I thought.

The miners looked at each other and nodded, it was good advice."

"When Larry saw the huge gold nugget, floating above the mule he blinked and shook his head then said. "What the devil? If you're trying to pull something on me, I'll shoot you deader than graveyard dead." He slipped the shotgun under his arm and started to untie the buoyant nugget. He smiled when it came loose in his hands. "Well I'll be!" He exclaimed as he walked back towards Joe and past the lead mule."

"As soon as he was clear, I took my shot, right through one of the feed bags. It started to whip around as one of the pancakes started its whoopee-dupe and rapped the rope around the robber's neck. Joe pulled out his belly-gun and shot the other bag that did the same thing, only in the other direction. As the gold lost it's flotation it crashed to the ground, pulling Larry Loud with it. I heard both ankles pop, as he fell. *Now* he wasn't smiling. The shotgun discharged, as it hit the ground, blowing the heel off his right boot. He let loose a terrible howl that shook the pine needles from trees miles away."

"His troubles were just beginning. We hog tied and blindfolded him. Next we strapped him to one of the mules for his trip to Grants Pass, and Sheriff Ketchem's jail. There was a reward for his capture, dead or alive and we planned to collect that as well as the commission for transporting the gold."

"I almost forgot, last time he had been captured he started to yell so loud Sheriff Pokey Smith let go of his six guns so he could but his fingers in his ears. Larry got the drop on him and escaped. I told Joe we had better gag this varmint or he might do the same thing to us."

"There was still some daylight left, so after building a fire and cooking some replacement hotcakes, to float the gold, we were on the trail again."

*   *   *

"The shadows were growing long across the trail and the first cool breeze of the evening told me it was time to make camp. Joe had bagged a couple of grouse as he led the pack train out of the deep Rogue River canyon and I was so hungry I could already taste'em. I yelled at Joe to stop at the next likely looking camp spot and he said he already had one in mind a little ways ahead, by a small creek. I smelled smoke about then and the undeniable odor of bacon frying."

"We halted the mule train and both Joe and I walked ahead cautiously with our shooting irons at the ready. As we entered the little clearing there was a woman bending over a campfire stirring a frying pan. We were close enough to hear the bacon sizzle. She had one of those sun-bonnets on and the brim nearly covered her face. We both holstered our six guns, as I said, "Hello the fire.""

"She didn't seem startled; she waved us in and kept on cooking. *Something didn't seem right,* but I thought, *I'm just a little nervous because of the gold and everything.*"

"As I stood across the fire from her, she looked up for the first time. Now I've seen some ugly women in my day, but this one would have looked better if she'd been struck by lightning. Then she spoke, "Like to have some fun old man?" The ugly face cracked in two with a big grin."

"We'd been had! It was Little Meaney and where ever he was, Big Meaney could not be far away. A voice came out of the shadows, "Throw down your things - err and leather stuff. I've got the fall on you."

"No! No! Darn it! I've got the *drop* on you, how many times do I have to tell ya? It's the *drop*." Little Meaney shouted, as he began taking off his disguise. Then he looked over at us, standing with our hands raised."

"Do you mind?" He said, with a toss of his head, as he started to slip the dress off."

"Joe and I both turned around with our hands still raised. We both realized we been had again and turned back to see Little Meaney doubled up with laughter."

The miners all roared as they visualized the little bandit dressed up in women's clothes.

"It didn't take much to figure who was the brains of the outfit."

"Joe and I both dropped our gun belts; this was getting to be a bad habit we'd picked up."

"We'd heard stories about the two robbers for years and all the jobs they pulled, and how they messed them up. One time over by Grants Pass they were going to hold-up the stage coach in the winter time. The stage was an hour late on a really cold windy day. As the coach got to the top of the pass they were going quite slow after the long steep grade, the driver saw two desperadoes, with their guns drawn standing in the middle of the road. The driver stopped the horses' barely in time and waited for the robbers to say something. They only stood there and then he realized they were frozen stiff, with icicles hanging off their beards."

"Whip'em Willie, the driver and the man riding shotgun, just picked 'em up and moved 'em to the side of the road. As they drove out of sight they looked back to see them still standing there with their pistols drawn. I'll bet they never lived that one down."

"Then there was the time over by Bandon when . . . well that's a whole different story. I better get back to my hotcake tale."

"Little Meaney, who was only about five feet tall, yelled at his little brother, who was well over six feet four, to pick up our gun belts and be quick about it."

"He looked at us and said, "Now where's that gold I been hearing about?""

"I said, "It's back on one of the mules. I'll go get it.""

"No you don't, you're trying to pull a fast one. I'll get it myself, my mom didn't raise no fools," Little Meaney replied."

"You're probably an orphan then," I said, under my breath."

"What's that? Are you getting smart with me? What did you say?" The man said, getting angry, threatening me with his revolver."

"I said, it's not 'ore then', it's been melted in to one big glob. Let me call the mule up that's carrying it and she'll bring it on up to you. O. K.?"

"All right but no tricks," he said, as he fidgeted with his pistol."

"I called to Rose and she came walking up the trail and stopped right in front of me and Joe, just as nice as you please. The big golden nugget floated above the mule bobbing in the evening breeze."

"This some kind of a joke?" Little Meaney asked. "Are you trying to pull something on me?" He walked over to the mule, holstered his six-gun, pulled out his pocket knife and carved a sliver of gold off the corner of the glob. Little looked it over real careful then put it in his mouth, bit it with his teeth and exclaimed, "It's really gold. What's going on here?" He stood on his tiptoes and reached up into the feed bag and started to pull out one of the hotcakes."

"I said, "I wouldn't do that if I were you."

"He looked at me defiantly and said, "You ain't *me*, old man."

"As soon as that hotcake cleared the bag it started to rise taking the little fellow with it. He was so startled he hung on, soon he was too high up to let go."

"Help! Help! Save me!" He screamed.

"I'd like to help, but I'm just an old man." "I yelled up to him as he kept going higher and higher."

Big Meaney was becoming alarmed, it must'a been like a man in a canoe watching his paddle float downstream."

"What did you do to my brother?" He sobbed, as he pointed his old cap-n-ball revolver at us. "Bring him back or I'll shoot ya."

"We can't bring him back, but you can join him if'n ya want too." I told him."

"OK, but no business silly," he managed to say."

"Come over here to this feed bag and take out one of these hotcakes and don't let go." I told him as I untied the rope holding the gold to old Rose and it settled to the ground. Joe reached up into the bag and handed Big Meaney one of buoyant discs. Joe took his revolver away and put one in his other hand. With a frightened look on his face Meaney's feet left the ground and he started to rise up into the air."

"What should I do? What should I do?" He shouted, in somewhat of a panic.

"Just hold on, don't let go and soon you'll be with your brother." I told him."

"Thank you," he shouted back."

"I almost felt sorry for the bumbling, big guy as he floated higher and higher towards his brother, who was now only a speck in the sky."

"Well the rest of our journey was uneventful; we arrived in Grants Pass a few days later and turned Larry Loud over to Sheriff Ketchem and collected our bounty. We had to wait till dark to leave the gold at the bank so no one would know how we transported it. They never did figure it out and we never told 'em," Roy smiled as he finished his tale."

"What happened to the two bandits that floated up in the air?" Matt asked.

"We heard rumors of an outlaw gang in Australia that pulled so many bonehead stunts it kept the local papers busy writing about them. There was a little guy and a big guy that led them. They never really had a 'G'd die'," Roy finished his story with a big laugh."

The miners all applauded the storyteller and asked for another one.

"Well you're out of pie and I'm out of time. We got to hit the trail early tomorrow morning to meet

Black Cloud in Grants Pass.   Next time I'll tell the one about, Flat Cakes." Roy told the miners. He looked over at Baldy and asked, "Are we invited for breakfast tomorrow morning?"

"Sure, Roy, but it won't be hotcakes," the cook laughed.

Chapter Twelve

THE UGLY HEAD OF INGNORANCE

The next morning as Roy and Matt were making preparations to leave the mine area Mr. Burrows asked to see Roy in his tent. As the old mule skinner entered he noticed about two dozen leather bags lay on the floor by the foreman's bunk.

"You know what you said last night about having gold on hand? It's true. I'd like you to take these sacks to the bank in Grants Pass, if you will and have them put in their safe. It might be best if we used a couple of empty flour barrels to transport them in and not say a word to anybody. Oh! And if you would, hold out a sack of gold to fill this list of food, goods and blasting powder, for our winter supply." He handed Roy a long list. "You can keep the balance of the sack. Could you do that for us old friend?"

"Of course Ben, I'd be glad to oblige you. I'll be back in a couple of weeks. I'll bring the mail too." Roy said.

"Oh! By the way B. C. found a body on the trail about a day south of here he had a tattoo of a whale on his arm. You ever seen a fellow like that?" Roy asked.

"That would be Moby, he used to work here, but I caught him stealing nuggets from the mine. He was a thief and if we had a trial I think they would have hung the scoundrel. It was about two or three weeks ago, I'm surprised he was still in the area. His real name was Richard Dicks, he was from the East Coast, used to be a whaler I'm told. It's not unusual for his kind to come to a bad end."

"That solves the mystery. Cloud is hauling his carcass to Grants Pass." Roy said.

A thought just popped into Mr. Burrows head, *Did Roy tell that particular tale, last night, so he would think about sending their gold to the bank? Hmm . . . he wouldn't put it past him. He was a crafty old codger.*

The miners were all milling around the entrance to the mine when Roy shouted out, R-O-P-E! Then R-O-P-E, TWO! All the mules came down the trail and lined up exactly as they had in the story last night.

Baldy shouted out from the cooking tent, "I don't believe this! That's a pretty good trick Roy."

The miners all laughed as they turned, lit their lamps and entered the drift. A few of them stood there with their mouths open, trying to separate fiction from fact.

Roy looked back and said, "Do I have to come back there and close your mouths for you?" His laugh echoed up into the box canyon and back, giving his departure an unreal quality.

*   *   *

Matt's legs were growing stronger and his endurance was becoming remarkable. He could walk all day without a rest. A few months on the trail with his uncle had made all the difference in the world. His attitude had changed from a surly, disinterested child to a capable youngster. He had learned how to build a fire, handle the mules, tie knots and track animals.

Black Cloud traveled with them now and taught Matt many Indian techniques in tracking, hunting and survival.

"Now look here he'd say, what kind of critter do you think this is?"

"Wow! That's the biggest deer track I ever seen," Matt, responded, dropping to one knee.

"How long ago?"

"I don't know . . . this morning?"

"Lucky guess Matt. See this blade of grass? It's still unbending so it must have been only minutes ago and if you look up you'll see your *elk* across that meadow."

The boy looked up just in time to see the tan hind end of a large elk disappearing into the thick brush.

"Big deer huh?"

It went on like that day after day. The old Indian pointing out leaves and shoots that had been nibbled, branches slightly bent and tracks over other tracks.

"It all tells a story lad, you just have to learn how to read it."

Matt was an eager student and learned quickly. When it came to rifle shooting he was even more enthusiastic.

"Now trigger pullin' is one of the most important things in shootin'." Roy said. "It's more of a squeeze than a pull though. You take the slack out of the trigger and then keeping your sights lined up and squeeze till she fires. Especially if you're using a muzzle-loader. It takes a little longer for them to go off than those new fangled brass cartridges. So keep your sights on the target till the smoke clears."

After instructions on how to line up the sights on his rifle he hit his first target. He was so excited he yelled and started to swing his rifle around to where Roy and Cloud were standing. He was surprised to find Uncle Roy right behind him stopping his movement. He grabbed his weapon and pointed it upright as he knocked Matt to the ground.

"I told you once I don't ever want to look down your barrel and find it pointed at me."

Matt was stunned that Uncle Roy knocked him down. The old man took the rifle and slid it into the scabbard on Evelyn then walked to the head of the train.

As Matt sprawled there on the ground mixed feelings stampeded across his mind.

Black Cloud offered him a hand up. "Don't take it too hard boy; he's just trying to teach you so you never forget."

"Well he didn't have to knock me down."

"Do you think you'll break anymore bottles when you're on the trail son?"

"No! Of course not." Matt said, looking at his scar.

"Do you think you'll ever swing your rifle around and point it at someone?"

"No of . . . I get it he did that so I wouldn't forget it . . . didn't he?"

"Yep Matt, he moved up behind you as soon as you started to draw a bead. He knew what you were going to do."

"He's not mad at me then?"

"No Matt, he's trying to instruct you in the only way he knows how. Now let's clean your rifle so's the acid in that black power don't eat up your barrel."

One of the most important techniques Matt learned was the ability to travel through the woods silently while keeping down wind of any game he chanced upon. He especially liked playing hide-and-seek at night with Cloud. The Indian always found him in a short time, but as the summer wore on he improved dramatically. Many times Black Cloud would be inches from his face before Matt would see him. An involuntary gasp would be muffled by the Indian's hand. Then Matt would laugh aloud, he was so amused by the game.

Cloud was also teaching him French and told him of his life when he was being schooled by French missionaries.

One day the old Indian took a vine and measured Matt's legs, waist, chest, feet and arms. The next morning he was gone without a word of explanation. A week later he was back. He had a bundle with him that he tied to one of the mule's packs and left it there until that evening's encampment. After supper he presented it to Matt. The lad untied the gift eagerly and held it up. It was a buckskin shirt and a pair of buckskin, britches.

"Oh! Thank you! Thank you! Uncle Cloud, this is the best gift I ever had." He immediately tried on the shirt and britches. A pair of moccasins fell out of the legs of the pants; the blue bead work matched that on the shirt. Then Black Cloud handed him a possibles bag made from a marmot pelt. Inside was an eight inch strip of heavy leather, about two inches wide with a one inch hole on each end.

Puzzled, Matt held it up and said, "What's this?"

"It's a socket for a tomahawk." Cloud said.

"But I don't have a . . . ."

"You do now," Cloud said, as he pulled a small tomahawk from his pack and showed Matt how to slip the socket over his belt and pull the handle of his new tomahawk though it. There was even a beaded cover made to slip over the sharp blade to keep it from cutting anything accidentally.

The exuberant youngster immediately pulled the weapon out and started his little happiness dance around the fire waving his new gift in the evening sky. The normally stoic Indian actually laughed out loud at the child's frolic. The two old friends sat there enjoying a glimpse into their own distant boyhoods, much different, but much the same.

"Did Mike Hammer make the tomahawk for you?" Roy asked.

Cloud nodded yes. "When I told him who it

was for, he didn't charge me for it. He said it was on the house, because he got such a boot out of your solution to the bonehead deputy problem. He said he still laughs every time he thinks about it."

"Good." Roy said.

*   *   *

Later Cloud showed Matt how to throw his weapon and had him practice everyday.

"When you're throwing at a target, let's say the knot on that dead tree, aim for the center of the knot. Not just the center of the knot but the very center of the center. And don't be satisfied till you hit it. One more thing; look at what you're throwing at and follow through. Now a tomahawk is going to spin around in the air as it flies to the target. You don't pull back on the handle to make it spin different for every distance, you find out what your distances are and throw accordingly. Like four feet, eight feet, twelve feet and so on."

As the little mule train traveled along Matt would pick out a target up ahead and throw his tomahawk then retrieve it as he passed by. After a couple of months with coaching from Black Cloud, he became quite accurate, even deadly.

*   *   *

One day weeks later after they had made many trips up and down the Rogue River and several of its' tributaries, they were dropping into the small town of Rogue River, a little south and east of Grants Pass.

There was a new trading post called Pete's Place

which Roy thought they ought to visit. Maybe the store would have some bargains, Roy always like bargains. He told Matt, "A bargain's not a bargain it you don't need it." A lesson in practicality.

The main street was hard rutted dirt and a mite dusty. They left the mules and horses all in a string, standing outside the store as the three of them approached the establishment.

A large freight wagon was almost finished unloading as two sweaty swampers struggled with a heavy barrel. The wagon started to move away from the loading dock, when the barrel came off the wagon. Roy jumped up and put enough pressure on the brake to keep it from becoming a disaster. The two burly men nodded their thanks to the old timer.

As the trio entered the store the proprietor looked up with a big smile that instantly turned to anger.

"Get out! I don't allow no stink'n redskins in here," He shouted, as he saw Black Cloud come in behind Roy.

Roy turned on his heel and started to leave. He usually avoided conflagrations with bigots and bullies. You could never change an ignorant man's mind; they had to do that for themselves. His money spent anywhere, no use in dealing with a disagreeable character.

"No! No! Not you mister, you're more than welcome, but not the no-good Indian and half-breed kid," the shopkeeper said, as he spotted the long list in the old mule skinner's hand.

Matt stood there perplexed, in his buckskin outfit and outdoorsman's tan looking more Indian than white.

Roy spun around his face dark with rage. His tomahawk in his hand quicker than the eye could see. Cloud tried to grab his arm, but he shook it off and was by him in a flash. He grabbed the surprised owner by the apron and pulled the much bigger man across the counter.

He pressed the blade to the panicked man's adam's apple and said in a terrifying voice, "Do you want me to peel this for you or are you going to apologize to my good friends, you pasty faced eastern whelp? If there were ten of you to stand by me in battle, I'd pick one of him over you or a thousand like you."

A foul smell emanated from the man stretched across the case, as a trickle of blood dripped to the counter.

"You're not even man enough to hold your bowels let alone to hold your place in a battle line." Roy said, cooling down a bit.

"Now apologize . . . no don't - don't - you're not good enough to apologize to my friend." He shoved the man back across the counter where he collapsed on the floor sobbing.

The freight wagon driver that had been talking to the storekeeper put his hands palms out and backed away, saying, "I don't want any trouble, mister." He didn't want any part of a crazy old man.

Roy didn't even notice him. As Roy went out the door he turned and said, "A bit of advice, go back to wherever you came from and stay with your own kind."

*   *   *

It was the middle of September and a few rain squalls signaled the beginning of fall.

Black Cloud had left a few days earlier to visit Dancing Flower, taking Matt's thanks with him for such an outstanding gift.

"You know school's going to start in a couple of weeks and were going to have to head out for the Murphy's ranch soon." Roy said, as they walked along ahead of the mule train.

"Couldn't I stay with you? I learn more talking to you than I will in school." Matt pleaded.

They walked in silence for a long time, Matt thinking about the Murphy place and all the children there. He realized he hadn't thought about them much in the last three months. *I wonder what Cat's doing? I wonder if she ever thinks about me.*

"Do you think they ever got that 'Old Three Toes,' you know . . . the cougar?" Matt asked.

"Maybe."

"Do you think they ever got a dog?"

"Maybe."

"Do you think I could have a dog? just a small one." Matt begged a little.

"First of all, if you have a dog at the Murphy's, it has to be with Lisa . . . Mrs. Murphy's say so and if it chases sheep it will have to be destroyed. That's a hard fast rule in ranchin' - no exceptions. And if it's for protection it can't be a small dog . . . they're too yippy anyway."

"If I have to go to the Murphy's I think I should have a dog." Matt stated.

"Ha! Ha! Ha!" Roy laughed, "So you think so, do you?" amused at the lad's spunk. "We'll see what we can do about it."

"I really would rather stay with you Uncle Roy. I like sleeping out under the stars and learning from you and Black Cloud. I feel as though he's my uncle too."

"Well the time will go fast, you'll have a good time at the ranch and it'll be Christmas before you know it. And let me tell you, Christmas at the Murphy's is an *event*. I'll probably show up about then and we'll have a real celebration."

Then one spring day you'll be sitting in the classroom, with the windows open. It'll be bright and sunny outside and that smell of summer stirring on the breeze. You'll be daydreaming about hiking up the old river and there will be a knock on the door. It'll be me and Cloud and the three of us will be heading out on another adventure."

The End

"Oh! And your dog will be
barking, eager to be off.

TUNE BACK IN...

In the next adventures of Rogue River Roy
and Matt Mc Coy, young Matt is on his own in
the vast wilderness of Oregon. Wins and loses
the love of Cat Murphy, defies his uncle
and joins the Rough Riders. Roy tells several
of his famous tall tales and captures a
dangerous outlaw. It's as much fun as an
apple shooting cannon.